Inn the Everlasting Vacancy

A Novel

RONALD GOODMAN
Springfield, Missouri

Inn of the Everlasting Vacancy

Cover and Interior Design by Scribe Freelance
www.scribefreelance.com

ISBN 978-0-9760040-7-3
Library of Congress Control Number: 2014904311

Published in the United States of America

NOTE FROM THE AUTHOR

Forty years ago when I first became interested in writing I cut my teeth on essays, none of which were actually fit to be published, I now consider in retrospect. One was published, however, in a periodical so obscure that I can no longer remember its name—sort of—thank goodness, lest somebody search archives and read the awful thing. I lacked the analytical mind (not to mention language skills) for parsing in such an acute manner that good essay writing demands.

I hadn't been embarked long upon my dream of being a writer when I heard the siren's call to fiction. Having grown up in America's heartland, Missouri, and spending a good many childhood days in the Ozarks where storytelling is as natural as allergic sneezing in a field of wild flowers, I knew that I had found my element, however modest my talent—if any—may prove to be.

Somewhere along the way in sharpening literary tools I came to believe that a story should be told for the sake of storytelling. If you want to preach, become a man of the cloth, I might have told myself. If you want to make statements, become a propagandist. If you want to be a storyteller, however, leave your grips and opinions out of it.

These days, forty years down the road from when I first penned a sentence of fiction, I still believe, pretty much, in storytelling for the sake of storytelling. I'm thinking of late, though, that there is no such thing as *pure* storytelling, as I'm interpreting pure in this context. The author is going to do a bit of preaching, whether or not he or she realizes it, if only disguised in satire. Moreover, a reluctance to go toe to toe with moral issues in the midst of storyline (if only on rare occasions that doesn't gain the author an absolute reputation as a writer of tracts and nothing more) that begs a storyteller to flog evil and injustice may amount to literary cowardice. A young aspiring writer once asked a Pulitzer winner what he thought was the most significant change in literature, or something to that effect, in his time. "The purists are tired," said the author.

"Tired of what?" came the follow up.

"Tired of being pure; if it works, it works." Though that author may not agree entirely with my own interpretation of *pure* in a literary sense, I have nevertheless—at least in this novel—drawn a purist line in the sand and crossed it myself.

RONALD GOODMAN
December, 2014
Missouri Ozarks

For those whose vacancy remains.

Inn of the Everlasting Vacancy

One

There's a beloved old adage that says "Only time can heal a broken heart." Properly, I might add. If in fact the heart in question *can* be healed, time is probably the best course of treatment. It requires no medication, usually, unless one is locked in the teeth of something nearing clinical depression, that is to say unable to eat or sleep, among other dysfunctions. It's a murderously painful route, though, for the patient is on the operating table 24/7 and under Father Time's knife for about two years on average. I speak not as a broken heart surgeon, but one who is himself writhing in pain upon that cold, stainless steel table. If anything could possibly be worse than my romantic system lying pretty much in ruins, it's the stupidity I feel for having gotten myself into such an emotional fix in the first place, and at my age, which I'll not divulge, for now. Well, I will admit that I've reached middle age, more or less. I think it's not geezerhood, just yet, but I'm not taking it particularly well. I can't seem to stop looking at the back of my head where a thin spot won't go away. Worst of all, in terms of hair, is the hairline, receding, which I must face every waking moment.

I'm admittedly something of a lone wolf; I prefer to suffer deep in the timber and to be left alone while licking my wounds. But after a year and a half of unrelenting agony, I decided that it was time to stumble out of the woods and talk to a friend. Let's see, I wonder who would best fit that bill, I thought. It didn't take me long to decide on Millie, owner of Tavern on the Gasconade nestled deep within central Missouri's Mark Twain National Forest where, in fact, I live these days. Having retired from my column on *The Kansas City Star*, I built a cedar log cabin along the banks of Roubidoux Creek in Pulaski County.

I thought it would be best if I called upon Millie at closing time, for the tavern is quite a popular watering hole and Millie doesn't relegate much footwork: she waits tables, works the bar, helps in the kitchen, and takes out trash, to name only a few of her self-appointed duties. She's also a better than average armchair therapist, I should note, and she doesn't charge for her services. In fact, she'll throw in a perk or two in the form of a glass of beer and some munchies to keep the patient talking.

It was *2:00 a.m.* when I knocked on the locked door. Millie parted a curtain and peeked out. She smiled and opened to me. "You've got things a little backward haven't you, Evan?" she said, ushering me inside.

"I'm sorry to bother you at this hour," I said, "but I need to talk to someone."

"Get in here boy, I'm all ears," she said. Millie does have rather large ears. She said that the older she got, the bigger they seemed to get, though she didn't know if her head was shrinking or her ears were growing, maybe both; double jeopardy. Whatever the case, she said that she was afraid to go out in a wind for fear of taking off then losing power and nose diving into the cold waters of the Gasconade.

We took a place at the bar and she drew each of us a draft. We sampled our beer then Millie said, "Alright, spill the beans."

"There was this woman I met a year and a half ago," I began.

"Ah, yes, a woman," Millie said, clucking her tongue.

"I was working on a story for the *Star*, a little urban renewal thing, and I kind of casually introduced myself while she was tending her flower garden."

"Ah, yes, the old flower garden syndrome," Millie said, sampling her beer once more and reaching for some peanuts sitting on the bar.

"This isn't funny, Millie. I'm really hurting."

"I'm sorry, Evan," she said, touching my hand.

"Anyway, I was in and out of her neighborhood for about six weeks, on and off. We kept running into each other. On one particularly hot day, she invited me to have iced tea on her back patio. She liked to sit close to me. We talked about a lot of things and I really enjoyed her company. She invited me to come for breakfast some morning. We set a date for the next day, actually. She called me early on the morning that I was to show up at her home and left a message on my cell phone saying that something had come up. She wanted me to return her call so that she would know that I got her message and wouldn't be coming over."

"Things do come up, Evan," Millie said.

"That's what I suspected."

"That's not what I meant," Millie said, glancing at me while a smile played at the corners of her mouth.

"I know, but she sounded funny and I thought that she probably had a man there, or at his place—calling me on her cell phone—and didn't want me coming over. Anyway, I never heard from her again and I avoided her neighborhood."

"So this is what's causing you so much pain?" Millie said.

"Pretty much. I knew that if she was with a man, it was none of my damn business anyway. And we hardly knew each other. But it hurt like hell. I was so God-awful lonely and there was something about her for me. I just melted down and self-destructed. It's been a year and a half and I go to sleep thinking about her and I wake up thinking about her. It's the greatest sense of loss of something I never had that I've ever experienced in my life."

"So, was she beautiful?" Millie said, pushing a bowl of peanuts my way which I declined.

"No. She was attractive, kind of little and quiet, haunting dark eyes and a beautiful smile."

"I'm assuming that you didn't sleep with her. Did you kiss her?"

"No. We touched hands once—well, twice."

"Wow!"

"You're still making fun of me, Millie."

"I'm not. My God, you're just so innocent. I think there's more to this than what you're telling me, Evan."

"She—uh—threw me a perfect pass and I dropped the damn ball."

"Now we're getting somewhere," Millie said.

"I wanted her to call my number in the huddle *one more time* and let me go deep for a bomb in the end zone. I'd go up in triple coverage and come down with the goddamn thing this time! I think she sent another dude downfield in my place."

"Male ego is scary, Evan."

"I know, but we're stuck with it."

"I think you made too much of this. You're a good looking man, Evan. A lot of women would love to get something going with you. If I weren't such a wrinkled, dried up old woman with her tits halfway in Mexico I'd get you into bed and put you in tune with nature."

"You were a hottie, Millie," I said as we both laughed.

"I could put a smile on my man's face when the lights went out; he'd be wearing it in the morning, too."

Millie refilled our glasses then fetched some popcorn from one end of the bar. "Eleanor Roosevelt once said that the best men still have some little boy in them," Millie continued. "The little boy in you, Evan, got you into one hell of a schoolboy crush that you probably had no business letting happen."

"Easier said than done," I said, sampling some popcorn and washing it down with beer.

"Here's my bottom line," Millie said. "Do you want to hear it?"

"Yes."

"I think that you've lost nothing but a fantasy."

I left Millie's Tavern on the Gasconade feeling better, if only for having talked to someone besides myself. My old friend didn't have any easy answers. Learning that I had perhaps lost nothing but a fantasy didn't ease the pain much, right off, but in days that followed it did seem to settle in.

I've passed the two year mark now, nearing three actually, and I'm considerably less obsessed with what I feared was my last best chance at love. I've been wondering of late, though, if love and romance will ever come my way again.

I've hit the big Five O. There, I said it. When I was in my forties I thought I was superman; all I had to do was flash the S in the form of hair on my chest and woman came out of the proverbial woodwork. I think it had less do with me being all that handsome—I'm a fairly average looking guy, in spite of Millie's stroking—and more to do with the predictable women who were attracted to me: virtually all of them were divorced with their desirability clocks ticking, so they thought. Their butts were still hot and the last thing they wanted was to be left out in the cold with a rather nubile fanny turning blue in an unforgiving singles wilderness where the wind never quits blowing.

The years kept rolling past, like the Missouri bent on its rendezvous with the Mississippi. And I'm as alone as I've ever been in my life. Curiously enough, spending the holidays with none other than yours truly doesn't bother me much anymore. It's Valentine's Day that does a number on me. The torture begins a couple of days early when I see guys and gals buying candy, cards, and flowers for their sweethearts. They'll have a nice dinner together tonight, out or at home, I'm thinking. Then later they, well … that's between the two of them. Each year Mr. Valentino punches me a little harder. He knows I'm not as emotionally resilient as I once was. Blows to the head and body hurt me more and staying on my feet takes some doing. I've been all but down for the count a time or two, barely managing to find the ropes and pull my battered self upright before the ref's counting ended in my loss. The heavyweight Jack Dempsey once said that a champion is somebody who can't get up, but does. I'm nobody's champion, but that line from the likes of Dempsey inspires me. This particular year was the worst. And as I watched that day make its dreaded approach, I could swear Valentino was throwing half eaten chocolates at me. I asked myself—for the first time ever, I think—this question: When is the last time a woman wished me Happy Valentine's Day, let alone give me a kiss and a card? I couldn't begin to remember.

When that day did indeed arrive right on time, I drove to a McDonald's to douse my self-pity with coffee and free Internet. I decided to park on the far end of a nearby Walmart lot, less traffic to dodge, and walk the short distance to McDonald's. Schlepping along a grassy area near the curb, backpack slung over one shoulder, I must have looked about as forlorn as I felt, and homeless as well. I'm one of those people whose face and eyes telegraph *all* that's going on inside. When I approached a drive and was about to cross, two women in a van stopped. The driver ran her window down and said, "I have a question." I thought she was going to ask for directions. She held up a large milkshake and said, "Sonic has a special today, buy one and get the other one free. My daughter already has something and I'm wondering it you might like this one."

"Sure," I said, trying to sound upbeat. I stepped to the van and she handed the milkshake to me. It was a huge thing, the color of Valentine with whipped cream and a cherry on top. I thanked her for it.

As she drove away, she looked back and said, "Happy Valentine's Day." I'm glad she continued on, for I didn't want her to see my eyes at that moment. She'll never know the good she did that day. I was far from being her sweetheart, of course, and she didn't even know my name. Random acts of kindness, someone has dubbed it, are more value packed than McDonald's Dollar Menu. I hitched up my backpack and continued on to McDonald's feeling like a stud, for a while, anyway. Getting through the rest of the day—without more virtual pelting of chocolates—would suit me, however.

The good woman didn't know that I'm a writer, it wouldn't have mattered anyway. And had she known that I'm a one book wonder—unless, of course, the muse whispers in my ear once more during the wee hours some fine morning—it would have mattered even less. I got lucky, though, after retiring early from *The Kansas City Star*. The book was published for the holidays that year, five years back. Its title, *You May or May Not be Crazy*, wasn't exactly something to be served with a cup of good cheer while sitting about one's Christmas tree—a shot of Jack Daniels, perhaps—then again, maybe it was. It flew off the shelves the day after Thanksgiving and kicked butt through the New Year. The first royalty check from my agent was a ticket to move out of my roach trap apartment and build a cedar log home on central Missouri's Roubidoux Creek. Since its publication, the book has had an odd way of cooling off then heating up again before it has really cooled, like young lovers whom Mother Nature has gone overboard with estrogen and testosterone. My publisher thinks that the book's popularity has something to do with the state of the economy. She thinks the world is under more constant economic pressure than ever before: inflation; deflation; gasoline prices up 15 cents a gallon in the span of two hours, than down 2 cents the next day. Milk prices seem to be dueling with gas to see who can produce the most radical swings. Job security has long sense been a thing of the past. All this volatility is sending people up a banana wall ... bananas are holding at 54 cents a pound, however, in my town. Grocer has a contract at that price, for now, I suppose. I recently saw a study claiming that having to always worry about money, even where one's next meal might be coming from, can lower IQ as much as 3 points or more. The ever widening gap between rich and poor is making some of us dumb as rocks. And the gap appears to no longer be just between rich and poor, as one writer said: it's between the rich and the rest of us.

I'm a writer of modest talent. But my book obviously touched a nerve. Curiously enough, I've no training or expertise whatsoever on the book's subject: hearing voices. The idea was born out of my own experience on three occasions, the first one being extraordinarily remarkable. I was house-sitting for a friend who had recently died. On the second night after her death, I was sleeping on a couch in a den just down the hall from her bedroom where she had drawn her last breath. In the wee hours of the morning, around *3:00 a.m.*, as I recall, I was drifting in and out of sleep when I heard her speak my name in a clear, level voice and coming from the direction of her bedroom. I rose up on one elbow, quite awake at that moment. She called my name again in the same level voice. It got a little scary at that point. After a few minutes of trying to gather my wits, I ventured down the hallway. I looked into her bedroom and half expected to see her. I saw nobody nor did I hear her again. So real was her voice that I actually looked under her bed and in a closet or two seeking a tape recorder, though I had never known her to be a practical joker. Had she been so inclined, I doubt that something post-mortem would have occurred to her.

The second instance, curiously enough, happened while I was house-sitting for another friend. She was an older lady who had lost a twenty-six-month battle with cancer. I was sleeping in her finished basement. It was in the month of February and the basement was a bit cold. I had my head covered with a blanket. Again, in the wee hours of the morning, my name was called out, "Evan, Evan, Evan." This voice wasn't quite as clearly identifiable as the first one, but I believe it was that of my friend. I snatched the cover from my head and answered. I received no response.

The third occasion, not so long ago and a couple of hours after midnight as in the other two instances, was more like the proverbial *small, still voice*. My name wasn't called this time, only the words, and spoken very softly in my ear: "Yes, I know how lonely life can be." When I rose later that morning, it occurred to me that what I had heard were words from a Don McLean song. Throughout the day I sang as much of it as I could recall. It comforts me still from time to time.

Though I never consulted a shrink, I suspect that he or she would explain it away as merely in my head. Had what I heard been *inside my head* I might have tended to be in agreement. At any rate I had no explanation then and I have none now. I heard what I heard. I have a theory, though: perhaps friends and loved ones have a capacity to leave behind a gift of embossing their voice—or, image upon a magnetic or radio wave that we can plug into for comfort, if only once. But one must have ears to hear and eyes to see, so goes another biblical passage from somewhere, the New Testament, I think.

I really meant for the book to be a satire directed at shrinks, many if not most of whom, I think, attribute voice-hearing to psychosis, if only in its early stages. For the sake of my own mental credibility in the eyes of the most rational among us, I might be wise to say that I never heard voices again. That wouldn't be true. I'll tell you about it a little later, hoping that you're not a shrink who has no patience whatever with us mystic souls where spirits have the giggling time of their lives.

Back, for a moment, to my wobbling sense of manhood. It had me in an awful quandary for a while, but I've come to a satisfactory conclusion: I wasted a lot of good love, and now it's coming home to roost. It's gotten harder and harder to find, the chemistry, that is. If I sense chemistry, if only at a distance, most of the time the woman is married or has a boyfriend; her chemistry is shared with someone else. And that is something I've never had a penchant for attempting to violate, even if given the opportunity. My greatest fear these days is that love may never come again. Damn it, Cupid, string your bow and put my name on some of those heart-tipped arrows and let 'em fly, you bare-assed little love monger. Give me another chance! I'll do better next time, I swear!

In the absence of arrows zinging through the air on my behalf, I decided that, in addition to setting myself up with a cozy hideaway along the banks of Roubidoux Creek, I should spend some of my book's money on a new truck; nothing like a new pickup with big wheels and high off the ground to make a man feel like he's more than he is. It wouldn't keep my feet warm at night or say hello to Captain Howdy, but it would have to do for now. There's something existential about a handsome truck; it's a kind of religion for a man. Washing it, down on one's knees polishing chrome wheels is worship time any day of the week.

I put a few things in a duffel, grabbed my laptop, violin case (the only thing Itzhak Perlman and I have in common is that we both belong to the human race), checkbook and headed out the door to my aging little SUV. It has some miles on it, doesn't use any oil, though, and starts in cold weather. That's a line I might apply to myself with the next female that shows at least passing interest in me.

The old jitney started faithfully. I put it in gear and we splashed across Roubidoux Creek with our sights set on Springfield and a Chevy dealer. That's when I heard the voice that has, in effect, changed the course of my life, as though the Roubidoux had suddenly begun flowing backward. Of course I looked this way and that to see if someone along the creek was speaking. I saw no one. I glanced at the radio to see if it was on. It wasn't. The voice came to me again, as if it meant to assure me of its reality: *A voice is heard in Ramah, weeping and great mourning, Rachel weeping for her children and refusing to be comforted because they are no more.*

The voice was level, but barely above a whisper, and I couldn't tell if it was male or female. I'm not particularly religious, but I knew those lines to be from the Bible, though I couldn't name the passage. I would fire up my laptop the first chance I got and look it up. Had I heard the voice only once, I might have easily dismissed it as some sort of disconnected serendipity moving through my brain's maze. Hearing it a second time and in such clear terms and outside my head stood the hair up on my forearms and the back of my neck. I thought that maybe I was being paid back for ridiculing shrinks: they've sent their clinical gods after me with oozing syringes in hand.

Reaching Springfield in the early afternoon, I sought out a dealership and spent no time bickering about price. The lot was well stocked and I found what I wanted. The truck would need some final servicing. I decided to spend the night in Springfield and pick up my new ride the next morning. I hadn't heard the voice again since crossing Roubidoux Creek, but I couldn't get it off my mind. I checked into a nearby hotel with free Internet and got my laptop going immediately upon getting to my room. I typed in the words that I had heard. Up came a number of versions from different translations. The verse was found in the Bible twice, the first being from Jeremiah 31:15. It was repeated again in the New Testament and the Gospel of Matthew. King Herod's order to slaughter infants in hope of killing the Christ child was believed to be a fulfillment of Jeremiah's words: *A voice is heard in Ramah, weeping and great mourning, Rachel weeping for her children and refusing to be comforted because they are no more.*

Whether or not that massacre ever occurred cannot be verified, by me, anyway, for I couldn't find it documented outside of the Bible. That isn't the point, I thought while shutting down my laptop. The words are poignant two thousand years later, it seemed to me as I wondered why I would be hearing what I heard. In 2008 the Center for Disease Control said that 3,000,000 reports of children being abused or neglected had been reported; six complaints per minute. How many of those complaints were legitimate may be debatable, but even one child abused by an abuser is not: upwards of four children die each day in this country from neglect and abuse. And that is a cold, hard fact.

I slept pretty well that night, in spite of my arbitrary linking of the Bible verse to child abuse, these two thousand or so years later. Notwithstanding my distrust of shrinks, dispensers of medication for managing the unmanageable, I think, I was nevertheless slightly concerned that I may be schizo after all.

The hotel had an excellent breakfast bar. I turned my attention to biscuits, gravy, and thoughts of my new truck. Short lived, that calmness of spirit, when I overturned my coffee cup upon hearing the voice again, a bit louder this time, it seemed to me as if the speaker thought that I wasn't paying adequate attention. A waitress came to my assistance, wiped up the spilled coffee, and refreshed my cup. I must have had somewhat of an alarming look on my face, for she asked me if I was alright. I said that I was; just a little clumsy.

It was the 15th of October when I decided to put a few break in miles on my Chevy Silverado. What a shot of machismo! I dared any dude to cut in front of my new wheels or delay me at a traffic light with his cell phone texting. I'd kick some ass!

Driving south out of Springfield, I picked up highway 160 and headed east. I had it in mind to explore some of Missouri's most rugged portions of the Mark Twain National Forest—keeping my new truck on the pavement, if at all possible—then turn around and return to my home on Roubidoux Creek. Where my head was when embarking upon an unfamiliar road, one of the most crooked on earth, I concluded, and a mere hour before dark, I'll never know while negotiating one serpentine curve after another. So sharp were some of the turns that I thought, once, I had seen my own truck go past. As darkness closed in, I considered turning back. That's when I discovered that I had somehow left hwy 160 and ended at an overlook where the road came to a dead end. Turning around and attempting to backtrack was a no brainer, not on these roads and in this darkness. I hadn't seen anything but an occasional set of headlights for 50 miles.

The upside to obviously having become lost, more or less, for the time being, was that I hadn't intended to make this a one day excursion. Before leaving Springfield, I bought a sleeping bag, ice chest, good flashlight, and Thermos which I filled with coffee at a convenience store. I stocked the cooler with salami, cream cheese for bagels, a quart of milk and orange juice. I set two gallons of drinking water in the bed of the truck. Loaf of bread, bagels, and a few bananas—if I'm going *bananas*, I might as well eat them—were on the backseat of the truck's extended cab. I decided to spend the night where I sat.

The moon was full this night, nearly so. It hung in the sky like a forsaken pumpkin too large for the patch. In this remarkable darkness even the stars seemed to keep their distance from the gargantuan thing that so dominated the night where I and my Silverado had come to rest.

Cutting the truck's engine but leaving the headlights on for the moment, I got out and had a look at my surroundings. Somewhere off in the hills I could hear hounds baying, hot on the trail of some poor something or other running for its life, I supposed. Where I had come to a stop was indeed an overlook. Massive blocks of limestone kept vehicles back from what appeared to be rather steep terrain; whether or not it dropped precipitously, I couldn't tell. I hoped it was a hundred feet straight down. If I hear that voice again up here, I'm jumping! Damn the shrinks and their vengeful gods. They can have what's left of me … a mere shadow of my former self. I love that cliché.

Returning to the truck's cab, I cut the headlights lest I become too conspicuous sitting there and invite bootleggers in need of a new Chevy and a little cash for upgrading their still. This trip was one moronic idea, I decided. I have no idea where I'm at and may not know much more come morning.

With the truck's lights off, my eyes began to adjust to the darkness. In the distance I could see a single light. How far away it was I couldn't guess. But I thought that it was coming from a house and on a second or third floor, given the light's elevation. I briefly considered trying to find my way to it. Missouri Conservation folk had confirmed the return of cougars (panthers, Ozarkers call them) to the Ozark Mountains. I wouldn't care to meet the glowing eyes of one of those cats on a narrow trail. Staying put and sleeping on the truck's seat seemed a better idea.

Becoming increasingly intrigued by the light in the forest, I decided to turn the truck around, fix myself a sandwich, and have a seat on the tailgate. Propping my feet upon one of the limestone blocks, I sampled my salami and considered the moon. It was a thing of beauty, even if it did deepen my loneliness. These big harvest ones have a way of doing that, I think. They aren't meant to be viewed solo. Hell, I might as well get my violin out and play something tear jerking. So long as I avoid bluegrass, which I do in fact love and play, any moonshiners that may be out and about will probably not be all that into Vivaldi. Retrieving the violin, I took up a bit of Vivaldi's *Four Seasons*. I played as softly as the instrument would let me.

I hadn't played long when I saw another light. It was in line with the light above it, but more at ground level. I couldn't tell if it was stationary or moving, so elusive was its distance in the darkness. I took another bite from my sandwich then returned to the truck's cab and found my Thermos. Coffee and I don't get along well in cool weather; it tends to roar through me. I drink it anyway. And this night relieving myself would only be a matter of opening the truck's door and pointing tally whacker in the right direction. It was getting cool out. It was eleven o'clock, I noted on my wristwatch. I snagged a hoodie then returned to the truck's tailgate, deciding against anymore music this night.

The moon hadn't moved much, pausing to look me over, maybe, wondering what I was up to. Perhaps it was a fan of Vivaldi, the Red Monk he was called with his great shock of red hair. He's been dead a couple hundred years, but his music lives on.

The second light down below was moving, I noted, drawing somewhat nearer. I believed it to be a lantern, given what seemed like flickering of a flame. If it was a bootlegger, there was probably only one of them, two at the most, seeing that there was only one lantern. I decided to return my violin to its case and stow it safely in the truck's back seat and retrieve a tire iron in its place and keep it handy.

Finishing the sandwich, I nursed my coffee and watched the light's progress. I was definitely going to have company. Whoever it was stopped for a time, perhaps reconsidering this visit, maybe a rock in a shoe, waiting for a panther to pass. The traveler resumed progress in my direction, however, and shortly I began to hear something, though not voices—thank God. How can I describe it? A jingling, tinkling. Wind chimes maybe. But the rhythm was much more methodical ... ice cream truck, out here and at this hour?

I lost track of the light, with the exception of its extended glow, and I could hear someone laboring up an incline out in front of me. Not a cliff, obviously. There was an occasional sound of metal bagging against metal. "Ouch!" I heard someone say. That someone was female, I deduced, given the tone and pitch of the voice. Whoever it was had reached the limestone blocks between me and them. I heard metal bang against stone, another "Ouch!" Then a head appeared. It was indeed a woman. She raised her lantern, blinked once, as if to get a better look at me then set the lantern on one of the stones. "Good evening," she said, smiling broadly, understandably out of breath.

"Good evening to you," I returned, thinking that unless she's got a tamed panther right behind her, she's one hell of a brave woman. I might be another Charlie Manson or Norman Bates sitting up here in the darkness.

"Could you help me up with my stuff?" she said, extending a hand to me. I reached and took her left hand. A kettle and little bell were in her right hand. She grunted in some exertion while I helped her reach the summit. "Whew! Thank you," she said.

"You're entirely welcome." The kettle was painted pink, I

noted. Something was written on it but I couldn't read it in the limited light.

She scooted the lantern to one side then sat before me upon one of the stones. She drew a deep breath, released it with a rush then crossed her legs at the ankles. She was wearing a red sweatshirt with something scrolled in cursive across its front. The lettering was worn and I couldn't make out what it said. The sweatshirt had ridden up a bit during her climb over the rocks and she pulled the hem down. "I saw your lights," she said. I only nodded. She set the kettle in her lap, took up the little bell in her right hand and rang it softly just once. "Would you like to donate?" she said, smiling again with what I thought was a remarkably even and beautiful smile. Her chin rose a little in anticipation of an answer.

"I—uh—sure," I said, reaching into a front pocket of my jeans and extracting a bill. I held it toward the lantern's light to see what denomination I was giving her. She extended the kettle toward me and I stuffed a five into the slot.

"Thank you, sir," she said, drawing the kettle back onto her lap. "God bless you and Merry Christmas," she added.

"And a Merry Christmas to you," I said, knowing full well that it was the 15th day of October. In addition to her sweatshirt, she was wearing jeans. Her feet were shod in hiking boots. There was an alabaster tone to her face, quite lovely, a fine oval, and almond shaped eyes appeared to be dark as nuggets of coal. There was a subtle but intoxicating scent coming from her. "I love that perfume," I said, stupidly, I thought, seeing that I had just laid eyes on the woman, didn't even know her name. You're a real Valentino, man, I scolded myself.

"I'm not wearing any," she said, uncrossing her legs then crossing them at the knees. My only response was to simply nod like something bobbing in a car's back window. A man's romantic tools get rusty hanging unused.

This woman wasn't a real talker and I was struggling to mitigate the awkward atmosphere. "Well, it's a lovely evening to be out," I said.

"Yes. I love this time of year."

Glancing at the kettle, I said, "So, do you get many donations, you know, out here?"

She shook her head slowly from side to side, blinked once and moistened her lips with the tip of her tongue. Whether or not her complexion was as exquisite as it appeared to be in the moon's light, I couldn't know. But the beauty of her throat made me wish that I were a vampire. Oh, to latch onto such flesh! So mesmerizing was her presence that I could almost hear the sound of bat wings. I looked to the sky for an instant, half expecting to see those creatures winging their way across the moon's face. For lack of something better to say, I decided I should introduce myself: "Evan Van Clevin," I said, extending my right hand.

She smiled and said, "That rhymes."

"Yes, and you're the millionth person who has noted that," I said.

"I wasn't making fun of your name."

"I know. I guess my parents were thinking I might turn out to be a rock star and would need something lyrical."

"Do you have a middle name?" she said.

"What?" I said, pretending not to have heard her correctly.

"A middle name, do you have one?"

"Yes."

"What is it?"

"Orbit."

I could tell that she was struggling to refrain from laughing out loud. "My father was interested in astronomy," I said.

"On my way here I thought I heard the sound of violin.

Was that your radio or a CD?" she said, changing the subject.

"It was me, I play," I said. "Not very well, I'm afraid."

"Vivaldi stuff?" she said.

"Yes."

"You should learn some bluegrass out here," she said, smiling.

"I know a few tunes, but didn't want to attract bootleggers."

She laughed then shifted the bell to her left hand and offered her right to me, "Rachel Mountjoy," she said.

My jaw must have come slightly ajar, for she gazed at me curiously for a moment. I collected myself and said, "Did you come from where the light is?"

"Yes, it's my house. It's not *just* a house, it's an inn. But nobody comes there."

"Do they not know about it?" I said.

"I guess they do. It's been in my family three generations. But there's no lane, anymore at least."

My visitor was silent for long moments. I saw sadness move through her dark eyes, as though she were recalling something unpleasant. She sighed, shifted herself upon the stone on which she was sitting. She rang the little bell once, looking at it as if she were pondering whether or not it was properly tuned then said, not looking up, "Do you like the sound of it?"

"I do. It's very Christmassy."

She looked past me at my truck then said, "Did you get lost?"

"More or less; I missed a turn someplace and ended up here."

"Are you going to try and find your way back tonight?"

"No, I'll sleep in the truck. I've got a warm sleeping bag."

"You can come for breakfast in the morning," she said.

"I'd like that."

"When you wake up, just head down the hill, it will lead

you to the inn. It's a ways, but the trail is good."

"It's a deal."

"Would you help me back down off this rock with my things, Evan?" she said, turning and preparing to climb down from the stone.

"Yes, of course."

With her kettle and bell in hand, I helped lower her to the ground and upon the trail then handed the lantern to her. "I'll see you in the morning," she said. "Just come when you're ready. I'll watch for you and get breakfast going."

"I'll be there," I said, wondering if she would call early in the morning and say that something had come up. She couldn't, of course, for she didn't have my cell phone number.

I watched her lantern's progress while she made her way back home. When the light went out in the inn, I put the tailgate back in place and returned to the truck's cab and unrolled the sleeping bag. I screwed the lid back on the Thermos and wondered if Rachel ground her own beans. Keep your head on straight with this woman, Evan, I told myself. She may ring *your* bell.

Two

I woke to the sound of a mockingbird and reached for my watch lying on the floor of the truck's cab. It was *7:00 a.m.* Dawn was just breaking. There had been heavy dew overnight and the windshield was coated. I turned the key in the ignition just enough to get some power to the wipers and hit them to clear the view. I heard the mockingbird again; what or whom it was mocking I couldn't tell. I know the sound of a mockingbird; there's one in my neighborhood on Roubidoux Creek. Beyond that, the only thing I know about birds is that robins' breasts are more orange then red, the female at least, it seems to me. I hadn't gotten undressed and only unrolled the sleeping bag to use as a comforter over me. Sitting up on the seat, I found the Thermos and poured a cup. It wasn't much beyond lukewarm, but drinkable. It would get a couple pistons firing for the walk through the woods to the inn. Running a hand across my chin, I thought that I could use a shave. I hadn't anticipated getting invited to breakfast on this trip. Splashing drinking water into my face to wash sleep from my eyes and brushing my teeth would have to do for now.

Having to sleep in semi-fetal position on the truck's front seat had left me stiff in the knees. I got out, stretched my legs, and nursed my coffee.

The mockingbird had taken a liking to me.

Beyond the great blocks of limestone that fronted the overlook was a vast wilderness that I couldn't have imagined in the darkness. I glanced at my new truck and wondered if Jack London would have liked it. Buck could ride in the back. Fall colors had not yet passed their peak. The panorama was breathtaking. With the exception of a chimney—Rachel's inn, I supposed—which was emitting modest smoke that curled away lazily, I saw no other   buildings as far as the eye could see. Early morning fog, waiting to be dissipated by the sun, hung in valleys like ragged sheets of gauze. It was Sunday morning and I could hear what must be a church bell, given its cadence. Awfully early for morning services, I thought. A little country church sending out a wakeup call to its flock: *"O let us go unto the house of the Lord."*

Finding a gallon jug of water in the truck's bed, I splashed water into my face then brushed my teeth as well. I looked into one of the side mirrors and ran a comb through my hair, locked the truck then mounted the stone barrier, lowered myself to the ground and took up the trail to the inn. It was a narrow path, scarcely enough room for two hikers abreast, and wound its way through timber so dense a man could scarcely lead a horse without difficulty. The trail was blanketed with fallen leaves, crimson, fading yellow, orange and a little green that hadn't yet been overwhelmed by the forces of fall. Acorns lying on the trail crunched beneath my feet. A curiously lovely display of death, I've always thought, decaying leaves losing their hold and falling to the ground: Mother Nature biding summer farewell and with an artistic touch of her brush. I had no clue as to how far I would have to travel before reaching the inn. Rachel said to follow the trail. That I was doing and with pleasure. I love the scent of leaves in the fall, especially when they are moist with dew or rain.

The mockingbird again, farther into the woods this time, seeking more responsive victims for its ridicule. A grey squirrel high in the top of a hickory fretted at me as it shredded a nut, spinning it between front paws with precision while cuttings showered down onto the forest floor.

The trail was descending at thirty degrees, sometimes dropping steeply for a short distance. Rounding a turn that circumvented a gigantic white oak, I could hear the sound of water, not rushing as if coming from a creek, but more of a trickling. I cast about and saw a cluster of limestone protruding from a bank ten paces off the trail. The face of the rock was wet. I decided to investigate and ventured from my path, navigating fallen limbs and a log or two until reaching the formation of rock. Water was coming from a crevasse and cascading in a tiny waterfall onto flat limestone then proceeding downhill upon a layer of moss covered stones just barely above ground. I cupped my hands and had a drink. The water was cold, as though it had coursed its way across sheets of underground ice before finding an outlet. I was not the spring's only customer: paw, hoof prints, and droppings told of other creatures having visited this place.

Returning to the trail, I continued on in what I thought was a southeasterly direction. I detected the scent of wood burning and guessed that it was smoke from the inn's chimney.

Having traveled another fifty yards, I suddenly broke from the tree line and into a clearing in the middle of which sat the inn. I must say that I was taken aback by what I saw. The building was two storied, for the most part; there was quite a lot of space above the second floor, a very large and accessible attic, perhaps. From where I stood, I could see only one chimney. I suspected that one or more rose from areas of the roof that I couldn't see at the moment. Some of the bricks on the chimney that was visible to me were missing and exposing crumbling mortar. Cedar shakes were dark with age but looked to be in decent condition, at least none were gone. The exterior was lap siding and badly in need of paint. Window frames wanted paint as well. None of the window's panes were broken, those that I could see from where I stood. A porch swing was hanging lopsided by a single chain.

Breaking from my cursory assessment of the building, I

strode across an assortment of decaying leaves and acorns strewn across the lawn then mounted a rather long flight of brick steps mottled with moss that led me to the inn's front door, a massive thing of ornately carved oak and in need of something, varnish, stain, perhaps, for its finish had blistered beneath the elements. On either sides of the door were copper lamps; glass was missing from one of them. I began to wonder if accepting the invitation to breakfast was such a good idea. There was something almost Hitchcockian about this house. Looking to a second story to see if Norman Bates' dead mother was sitting at a window crossed my mind. But upon stepping to the door and taking a heavy, lion's head knocker in hand and picking up the aroma of brewing coffee, baked or frying ham, the place seemed less menacing. I rapped on the door twice and waited for the sound of footsteps.

A brass door handle with more patina than it probably needed turned slowly and Rachel Mountjoy opened to me. "Good morning," she said. "I saw you standing at the tree line and wondered if you were about to change your mind."

"I was just looking the place over. It's—uh, very rustic."

My host smiled and opened the door wider to allow me entry. She stepped back and quickly looked me over from head to toe, scanning my bar code. I wondered what she had come up with, how I had totaled out. In the light of day I found the woman even more beautiful. Her chestnut hair was pulled back into a bushy ponytail and the subtle, varying tones showed no sign of having been colored. Eyes that appeared black as nuggets of coal last night were in fact dark brown with cashew around their irises. She was wearing jeans and a black and white checkered flannel shirt. Her feet were shod in newish looking sneakers. "Something smells good," I said, stepping into the foyer.

"How does ham, eggs, and biscuits sound?" she said.

"Excellent."

If I was taken aback by the inn's neglected exterior, and I was, the contrast of the palatial interior stunned me. Beneath my feet was finely finished, four inch walnut flooring in the middle of which was an area rug—if I may use that term for such obvious quality—of burnt orange and green. The foyer was half as large as my cabin on Roubidoux Creek, I thought as I took in my surroundings. Walls were papered in floral design of ascending shades of blue, purple, and grey. Judiciously placed abstract paintings of various sizes complimented the entrance.

Rachel led me on into the great room where I was met with more of the walnut flooring and exquisite rugs, frugal in number and size so as not to eclipse the walnut upon which they lay, I reasoned. The walls of the great room bore the same paper as the foyer and more abstract paintings were present. A fieldstone fireplace with copper hood occupied one end of the room. Furnishings were modest in number but ample, giving one a sense that the owner didn't like clutter. A Baldwin baby grand piano with its lid propped up sat in the middle of the room and easily dominated, so fine was its finish. The ceiling was vaulted into the stratosphere. Studio lights mounted on massive beams would illuminate the area below when needed. A staircase with walnut steps and banister made left then right angles while it sought the inn's second floor. I wouldn't hazard a guess as to how many board feet of walnut were in this building. The cost of such finished lumber would probably pay for my Chevy Silverado two or three times over.

"Biscuits are in the oven. I'll pour us some coffee while we wait on them," Rachel said as she led me into the kitchen where walnut flooring ended and inlaid stone began. Another fieldstone fireplace, much smaller than that in the great room, was in one corner of the kitchen. Mingled with the aroma of ham and baking biscuits was the scent of well seasoned hickory, banked quiet early, for the fire had burned to glowing, pulsating embers. My host added a couple sticks of wood. Flames soon began to lick what she had placed upon the grate. Being fond of wood burning fireplaces, I thought I detected a trace of apple wood that had been added to the fire, emitting a subtle sweetness into the air. The kitchen's walls were papered in burgundy pinstripe. Copper and brass were abundant. Appliances were stainless steel, commercial quality, suitable for the work of an innkeeper, I deduced. A Formica topped bar jutted a third of the way into the room and I took a seat upon one of its stools. "Do you use sugar or cream?" Rachel said.

"Just black," I returned. Sitting near the coffeemaker was a bag of Starbucks French Roast beans and a grinder. Rachel's kettle and bell sat on a table near a doorway that let out into what looked to be something of a screened work room, I guessed, with lots of wooden, unpainted counter space with stone tops for preparing things destined for the kitchen: snapping beans, cooling pies, preparing chickens, perhaps, and the like. Beyond the screens I could see what looked like a smokehouse. At one end of the table where the kettle and bell sat was a sewing machine. Lying beside it were scraps of fabric and a pattern. The remnants of cloth were the color of burlap but looked to be wool. Scissors were lying nearby.

My host poured coffee for the two of us then seated herself on a stool across from me. "The biscuits are about ready," she said. "The ham is done. I'm just keeping it warm. All I have to do is fix the eggs. How do you like yours?"

"Over easy." Tending my coffee and glancing at the kettle and bell, I said, "How long have you been with The Salvation Army?" knowing, of course that their kettles were painted red, not pink.

Sampling her own coffee and gazing at me over the cup's

rim, she set the cup down and said, "I'm not *with* them. I just think it's a neat thing they do, ringing the bell and collecting money for the poor. And they've been doing it for so long. Did you know that the first bell ringer was in San Francisco in 1891?"

"I didn't know that," I said.

"His name was Joseph McFee—I think the biscuits are probably done," she said abruptly. She went to the oven and withdrew the biscuits and checked their doneness with a toothpick.

"How did you come by the kettle and bell?" I said as she strode to a refrigerator in search of eggs.

"I found the kettle in a flea market. It was black. I painted it pink. A local man who does sheet metal work made the lid for me and cut a slot for money. I got the bell from a gift shop."

"They look authentic," I said. Then, "What is that written on the kettle?"

"Remember Rosie. I'll tell you about her sometime. They had them on ebay, The Salvation Army ones, but they looked kind of phony. Anyway, if they had something about Salvation Army on them, I might get sued. How embarrassing, getting sued by The Salvation Army!" She glanced over her shoulder at me while preparing our plates at a counter.

How long have you been doing it?" I said, noting how well her jeans fit.

"Doing what?"

"Bell ringing."

"A while," she said, bringing our plates of food to the bar.

"Has The Salvation Army ever complained," I said, taking eating utensils handed to me.

"Not really. I guess I had gotten kind of famous. One of their officers found his way here once and talked to me. I told him I thought I might be related to Joseph McFee, you know the first bell ringer in San Francisco I told you about. I'm so full of crap sometimes, Evan. Anyway, I don't have anything that says Salvation Army on it, so they can't stop me. I think he was interested in persuading me to send the money to them. I don't, though."

"What do you do with the money?"

"I send it to organizations that help neglected and abused children."

I didn't hear the *voice* that first spoke to me when crossing the Roubidoux, but it streamed across my mind like Wall Street ticker tape.

We ate in silence for a few moments. I heard a soft knock coming from the direction of the room off of the kitchen. I could see a child—young woman, actually, though she was dressed like a monk. She was standing on the other side of a screened door. "Excuse me," Rachel said, putting a napkin to her mouth then rising from her stool. The girl looked to be twelve or thirteen years old. There was a certain maturity to her face. The hood to her robe wasn't on her head, exposing a fabulous head of hair so blonde it looked almost platinum, going every which way, as if she had just emerged from a great wind. Her eyes, the color of which I couldn't tell through the screen, were large and somber. She gazed at me but said nothing. Rachel opened the screened door and exchanged a few hushed words with her visitor. The girl shook her head then disappeared into the forest. I wanted to ask who the visitor was, but thought that I had already been nosy enough.

Rachel regained her seat and took up her coffee cup. "That was my friend Hannah. She loves to sing while I accompany her on my piano. I asked her to come in, but she didn't want to. She's very shy with strangers."

"Is she a monk?" I asked, smiling with tongue in cheek.

"No. She asked if I could make her a monk's robe," Rachel said, glancing at the sewing machine. "I had a terrible time finding a pattern. It's not like we see people going around dressed like monks. I'm surprised some monastic order hasn't showed up and tried to recruit her," she said, chuckling. "Of course she's a girl, and I doubt that they would allow her mop of blonde hair in a nunnery."

"She's lovely," I said. "That looks like really nice material," I said, cutting to the sewing machine and remnants of fabric whose burlap color belied its quality.

"Yes, it's Merino hoggets wool, the finest. It originated in central Spain and Turkey. It cost me an arm and a leg, but I wanted her to have the best. She grew up terribly poor."

I wanted to ask where the girl grew up at but opted to break apart my biscuit and apply strawberry preserves to it.

"If you're in no big hurry to go home, Evan, you can stay here for a night or two——as long as you want, really. I won't charge you anything."

"I'd be a little afraid of leaving my truck at the overlook," I said. "You said there's no lane to the inn."

"Yes, no lane. But there is a way to get in here. It's an old wagon track, hardly anybody knows about it. I use it for my Jeep when I need to go to town."

"I had no real destination, just sightseeing. Leaving Springfield so near dark was a poor time to set out sightseeing," I said. "It's no wonder I made a wrong turn and found myself at a dead end."

"I know some good trails we could hike, if you like doing that," Rachel said, rising and fetching the coffeepot to warm our cups.

"Sounds like a plan, and I could use the exercise."

After finishing what was on my plate, my host said, "Did you get enough to eat?"

"I certainly did. The ham was delicious."

"It's from my smokehouse. I don't raise pigs but I buy a hog every couple of years and get it butchered then cure the meat."

"How long has it been since this inn has had any guests?" I said.

"About five years. It's been in my family for three generations, as I said last night. There was quite a lot of land with the property. I sold most of it. I kept a hundred acres around the inn so that I could have privacy. The lane that entered from the highway is grown over now, but there used to be a sign at the entrance. A big tree blew over in a storm and knocked it down. I never put it back, of course, since I decided I didn't want to be an innkeeper anymore." She warmed our coffee again then said, "Where do you live, Evan?"

"I have a place on Roubidoux Creek, near Waynesville in Pulaski County."

"What sort of work do you do?" she said, wiping crumbs from the bar's counter into the palm of one hand.

"I wrote for *The Kansas City Star*, community stuff, mostly. I sort of burned out on the subject ... got to feeling a bit reclusive, retired early."

"I once heard that Hemmingway wrote for the *Star*."

"He did. That's where he was taught to write short sentences," I said. "My sentences are short, but I'm no Hemmingway," I added, chuckling.

We finished our coffee and Rachel said, "Let's go get your truck."

Outside, I followed her to a shed at the rear of the inn where she collected a pair of pruners. "We might need these to trim a limb or two so they don't drag on your truck. My Jeep is old so it doesn't matter if it gets scratched."

Making our way up the trail toward the overlook, I said, "I

thought you were pretty brave coming up here alone last night."

"I carry a snub-nosed 38 in the kettle," she said.

"I see."

I had to extend my usual gate to keep up with my hiking partner. I'm decently fit for a guy my age, but I was sucking a little wind on the uphill climb. "It's more difficult than coming down," Rachel said, glancing at me and smiling. Then, "I'm being awfully nosy this morning, Evan, but how old are you?"

"Fifty."

"I'm forty-two," she said, taking my hand. "I love going for walks and hiking, but it's no fun alone."

The scent coming from her that wasn't perfume, she had informed me, I found even more intoxicating in the fresh morning air. Mother Nature has a penchant for excesses, I thought: so little for some, so much for others. *Yes, let us give our Rachel something extra to compliment her beauty, a natural scent gathered from exotic Isles yet to be discovered.*

Approximately halfway to our summit and hearing the sound of trickling water, Rachel said, "Are you thirsty?"

"No, but I did have a drink from the spring on my way down this morning."

"We're almost there," she said. "I see the top of your truck through the trees."

"I'm glad to hear that," I said. "I hope my ice chest is still there."

"Not much stealing around here," she said.

We reached the overlook and the two of us mounted the stones to where the truck sat unmolested. My ice chest was where I had left it. I unlocked the doors and opened for Rachel. "Where we need to turn in is about a hundred feet back down the hill," she said. "Go slow. It's not far. There's a big willow. Stop there."

"Got it," I said, starting the engine and pulling away from the overlook.

"Beautiful truck," Rachel said, glancing about the interior.

"Thank you. I'm awfully proud of it."

I eased along the road until seeing the willow. "That's the spot," Rachel said. "When you get there I'll get out and pull the limbs back and let you in."

Coming to a stop before the willow, Rachel got out and pushed the tree's tendrils back a bunch at a time while I slipped through with the truck. A few of the spindly limbs brushed the cab harmlessly. Once inside the hidden passage, Rachel came to the driver's side and said, "I'll walk ahead of you and watch for limbs that need to be cut back."

"Do you want to drive and let me do that?" I said.

"No, I wouldn't trust my driving with something so new."

I crept along the track while my guide walked ahead of me with clippers in hand, occasionally stopping to prune or drag a limb out of the way. The old wagon track was barely discernable, and that mostly from the opening among the trees. There were brief stretches where Rachel jogged ahead of me, waving me on when the track was straighter and clear of obstacles.

Rounding a turn and ascending to a knoll, I saw the girl again. She was gathering walnuts and depositing them into a gunnysack. She spoke softly to Rachel, words I couldn't make out. She only gazed at me with her enormous, somber eyes as I passed. She pulled the hood of her monk's robe onto her head. I waved but she didn't return it as she dragged the bag to another tree.

Rachel halted and let me catch up. Drawing alongside of her I said, "That girl gets around. Does she live nearby?"

"Not far," Rachel said. "We're almost there, just a little beyond that bunch of cedar," she added, pointing in the direction of the trees.

Breaking from the stand of cedar, it was a clear shot to the inn. My guide got back into the truck and rode the rest of the way. "Whew! It's been a while since I walked that trail," she said, toying with her ponytail and shooting a look at me."

"Nothing like a secret passage," I said, coming to a stop in front of the inn.

"My private entrance. Evan, do you think you want to be my guest?"

"I think I'd like that," I said.

I brought in my duffel containing a couple changes of clothes, toiletries, laptop, and violin case. Rachel informed me that the inn was wired for Internet. The items in the ice chest found their way into one of the kitchen's refrigerators. I was shown to a room on the second floor. The room was simple elegance, appropriately in line with what I had seen elsewhere in the house.

We sat in the great room and chatted for an hour or more, mostly about our personal lives, to a point. Rachel asked if I was married. I said no, not anymore, and that I'd been divorced forever, it seemed. She asked if I had any brothers or sisters and I said that I was an only child, born to my parents rather late. They were both dead. I was the father of no children—legitimate or otherwise. Rachel found that amusing. She herself was widowed five years. Her husband drank, too much, and was killed in a single car accident when he left the road on a dangerous curve and hit a tree. She had borne no children. She too was an only child born late to her parents. We had that in common, I thought. Having spent so many years in a busy newspaper office, I was struck by there being not one phone call since my arrival. A cell phone lay on the kitchen counter. The peace was palpable.

Rachel suggested that we have an early lunch then hike her favorite trail. And, too, there was someone she wanted me to meet.

Three

As a rule I wouldn't advise hiking in the Ozark Mountains shortly after a lunch of bacon (from Rachel's smokehouse) and tomato sandwiches—two of them for me—sweet tea, and blackberry cobbler with nearly a pint of vanilla ice cream on top. It can be done, however, and the two of us set out to prove it, even if we did burp for the first two hundred yards. Mid-October temperatures had moderated, of course, especially humidity which can hang over the great Ozarks plateau like steam above a bowl of soup. But the terrain knows nothing of temperature change and we sometimes had to grab hold of a sapling or tree limb to pull ourselves to a crest. The trail comfortably circumvented such inclines when possible, though not as frequently as I would have liked. I wondered who had cut the trail in its infancy, man or beast.

Since being invited for breakfast, one question hadn't left my mind: What is this woman's interest in me? When she had left last night and I lay down in the cab of my truck, I couldn't imagine that her first name matching the biblical passage could be anything but coincidence. That conclusion became blurred when learning that the money she collected in her kettle was sent to organizations that help neglected and abused children. More coincidence, perhaps, but I'm no match for her movie lot looks. I'm an average looking guy; not overweight; don't smoke; no drunk; and an acceptable bed partner, in my own estimation, if not exactly having heard a lover screaming—"Evaaan! Oh God! Evan, babyyy!" In the absence of such 7 point Richter scale quakes, have a look at a woman's eyes after making love. She may not have ripped the sheets from the bed, but if her eyes have that subtle, curiously *just woke up look*, then she was taken to where she wanted to go. Of course there could be another side to that sensual coin: if in fact she did simply *wake up* when it was over, a man must rethink his sexual prowess. What's more, if she reached for a cigarette while you were … disastrous, a most eliminating indication. Should the first observation be happily true, however, she'll be looking forward to another ride when the pony whinnies at her door. Somebody once said that sex is like housework; it never stays done.

Whether or not Rachel had anything romantic in mind was a question better left alone at the moment. I was enjoying her company very much. There was a quiet energy about her, something remarkably confident in those cashew laced brown eyes, as though she were the keeper of some great secret that could not be guessed and only she endowed with power to divulge.

My hiking partner had suggested that we take along a water bottle each, which she provided. We could fill them at a spring not far along the trail, she informed.

A few hundred yards into our trek, we came upon the spring. The water was oozing if not bubbling from the ground only a few paces from the trail. Upon closer inspection, I could see that limestone, barely breaking the surface of the forest's leaf laden floor, was the source from which the water emerged. The Missouri Ozarks has no shortage of natural springs. The Gasconade River, not far from my home on Roubidoux Creek, is said to have 70 some springs feeding it as it courses through 10 Missouri counties. The small stream at which Rachel and I now stood found its way downhill ten feet or so at thirty degrees across more or less flat limestone until interrupted by a pool, built of loose stones that collected—if only briefly—the clear, cold water. A tin cup hung from the limb of a nearby dogwood. Rachel fetched the cup and handed it to me then unscrewed the top of her water bottle and submerged it into the pool. "Mmm, good stuff," I said. She smiled then took the cup and got herself a drink while I filled my own water bottle.

"Me and Hannah built the pool," Rachel said, finishing her drink and returning the cup to its place. We took up the trail once more.

"Does she live in the neighborhood?" I said, knowing that I had asked that question before, only couching it in slightly different language, a kind of cross examination hoping to get a different answer.

My partner didn't respond. "Oh, look, a fawn and its mother," she said, pointing into the woods where the two deer were watching us. Not willing to risk tolerating much of our attention at such close range, the doe turned and bounded into the forest with fawn not far behind.

We hiked on for what seemed to me a considerable distance, mounting hills, circumventing great outcroppings of limestone bluff that allowed us to do so, some of which contained intriguing cave openings large enough to enter, and then dropping precipitously into ravines. My friend's hickory smoked bacon was exacting a price; I had gone to my water bottle shamelessly often. Though male ego wouldn't dare let me complain or breathe as heavily as I wanted to, I was ever so glad when she said, "It's not much farther. When we get to the top of that ridge up ahead where you see the grove of blue spruce, our destination is just a little ways on the other side."

Topping the ridge, we found a pleasant breeze moving through the boughs of the spruce. "Let's rest here a few minutes," Rachel said.

"Excellent idea," I said, lowering myself to a soft bed of pine needles and unscrewing the top to my water bottle. Rachel sat down as well. The opposite side of the ridge in the direction which we now faced ascended at forty-five degrees for thirty yards then leveled off into pasture where a half dozen white faced cattle grazed. The valley, something of a clearing, really, for it was encircled on three sides by forest and the ridge upon which my partner and I now sat, ended abruptly on its southeastern border by bluffs that rose eighty or ninety feet, I would guess. The face of the great wall of limestone was scared with cracks and pocked with cave openings. One of the caves was quite large. Though I had no clue as to how deep the cavern might be, I couldn't imagine any creature being able to scale the face of the bluff to gain entrance. I suspected that it was probably home to quite a colony of bats.

Not quite positioned in the middle of the valley was a house. It was one storied and built of mortared fieldstones. The roof was of terracotta tiles and hosted a single chimney emitting smoke that wafted lazily to the southeast. There were quite a number of paned windows in the home, giving one a sense that its owner wanted plenty of natural light and a view, in every direction, of the remarkably pristine homestead. A low porch fronted the home. An unpainted picked fence of cedar, I thought, encircled the property. "The person I want you to meet lives there," Rachel said.

"Gorgeous place," I said, going to my water bottle again.

"Her name is Moriah Hawkins," Rachel said. "She lives there alone. Nobody around here knows how old she is and she won't say. I think she might be a hundred. She has more wrinkles than a raisin. Her eyesight and hearing are remarkably good. Her voice cracks a little, but she's easily understood. She's God-awful smart and taught physics and cosmology at the University of Chicago."

"Jeeesus," I mumbled.

"She knew the physicists Hugh Everett who more or less introduced—or, made popular, in this country, at least—Parallel Universe theory. He died rather young at fifty-one and drank heavily, people said. Moriah thinks the theory probably drove him to drinking."

"I'm not surprised."

"Moriah has outlived two husbands. She gave birth to a stillborn child and never attempted another pregnancy," Rachel continued. "Her family owned this valley and she grew up here. Both of her husband's and the baby are buried in a cemetery just inside that tree line over there," Rachel said, pointing to the northeast. "People say she visits the graves every morning when the weather will permit."

"Let's go," I said, getting to my feet. "I want to meet this woman."

Our descending the ridge was not without difficulty. Quite a lot of scaly bark hickory grew on the slop and the nuts rolled beneath our feet. "Squirrels are falling behind with their work," Rachel said, chuckling when she nearly lost her footing. "I should come back and collect some of these," she said, stopping to pick up one of the nuts. "Have you ever had hickory nut pie?"

"Can't say that I have."

"It's good, kind of like pecan pie, has the same look."

Off the ridge and on more negotiable ground, we strode across a blanket of red clover and fescue, occasionally having to dodge a cow pile, some of which were fresh enough to suggest they not be stepped on. Nearing the house, we could hear the sound of hammering, not in rapid succession as though something were being built or repaired, but a single stroke or two at the most. "I think it's coming from the backyard," Rachel said, opening a gate in the fence then closing it behind us. I followed her and as we rounded the corner of the house we saw an older woman sitting at a rough-sawn, picnic like table. Her hammer was poised to strike another walnut lying before her.

Noting our presence, the woman laid the hammer down and turned to us. "Good morning, Rachel," she said, rising rather slowly from her seat on a bench and embracing her visitor.

"Good morning to you, Moriah. I'd like you to meet my friend, Evan," Rachel said, turning slightly to me.

"I'm pleased to meet you," I said, taking a hand so thin I feared squeezing it in the least.

"It looks like you're doing some fall harvesting," Rachel said, glancing at the walnuts spread on the table.

"I've wanted some walnut cookies with my coffee. The nuts are awfully good this year. Hannah brought me these early this morning."

Rachel took up a nut pick and began working the fruit from one of the shells. The old woman's cobalt blue eyes seethed with intelligence and they were fixed on me. "Are you a writer, Evan?" she said in a voice that cracked just a bit. She was wearing maroon cords and a heavy, charcoal colored sweater that hung on her slender frame. She crossed thin legs beneath the table and clasped her hands before her and waited patiently for my response, as though she had just sought an answer from one of her graduate students at the University of Chicago.

"As a matter of fact, I am—was, I should say. What made you ask?"

"The lines at the corners of your eyes and thoughtful way you tip your head. It reminds me of a writer I once knew. Were you fired from your writing job?" she said, chuckling.

"I quit. I wrote for *The Kansas City Star*, community stuff mostly … just got tired of writing about what other people are doing, so I packed it in early."

"Quitting a job is easier on one's pride than being fired," Moriah said. "Collecting unemployment can be a problem. It's best to have a nice nest egg before telling one's employer to go to hell." The old woman held my eyes for long moments then said, "What is your last name, young man?"

"Van Clevin," I said.

"And would you by chance be the author of that fascinating book, *You May or May Not be Crazy?*"

"I am."

Rachel ceased picking at the walnut and looked at me. "You didn't tell me that, Evan."

"Nothing more boring than hearing an author tout his own book," I said.

Moriah turned to Rachel and said, "Have you been doing much bell ringing, dear?"

"Not much," Rachel said, then clucking her tongue in difficulty with getting a nut to come loose from its shell. Then, "Oooh, that's a good one!" she exclaimed when finally dislodging the nut. She held it up for us to see. Moriah smiled and nodded. "I did get five bucks from Evan last night," Rachel said, returning to the bell ringing question. "He made a wrong turn and got lost on the overlook. I made him pay for his mistake."

"She's painfully shy isn't she, Evan?" Moriah said. "She knows how to work the angles."

"I couldn't say no. At any rate, I would have been afraid to had I known she carries a 38 in that kettle."

"Well, with her beauty she doesn't need a gun to get donations," Moriah said.

Rachel rolled her eyes then said, "You were quite a looker at the university, Moriah. Professors were running into doors all over the place."

"That's because their eyes were bad from too much reading. Anyway, I was married then and they had no business ogling me."

A Mason jar with a handful of daisies was sitting at one end of the table. Moriah saw me looking at them then reached for the bouquet and drew it to her, toyed with the blossoms and said, "Hannah brought these to me when she delivered the walnuts. Aren't they lovely? The frost hasn't quite gotten them yet."

"Awfully thoughtful child," I said, thinking that the girl was either strong as a Missouri mule or had a wagon. Her gunny sack appeared to be half full when we saw her earlier this morning. And it was one hell of a walk through the woods from where we had seen her gathering the nuts.

Moriah's eyes were fixed upon me once more. Her chin rose slightly as if she were about to ask a question. Instead, she turned to Rachel and said, "I'd like to take the flowers to the cemetery later. Would the two of you mind going with me? My arthritis is acting up today and I'm not all that steady on my feet."

"We'd be happy to," Rachel said, looking to me for concurrence which I gave.

"I've got a pot of pinto beans on. We'll have cornbread, too. I hope you'll stay for supper. I have pecan pie for dessert," Moriah said.

"Set the table for me," Rachel said.

"I'm in," I said.

A bowl containing a modest amount of the walnuts gleaned from their shells was sitting in the middle of the table. "Let's work on these nuts until we get enough for a batch of cookies then I'll help you bake them," Rachel said.

"I think I've got another hammer and a couple of picks in the house. I'll get them and bring us a glass of cider," Moriah said. Our host rose slowly from her seat and reached a hand to Rachel who accompanied the old woman into the house. They returned shortly with nut cleaning tools in hand and a carafe of cider and glasses as well. Moriah poured while Rachel and I took to shelling walnuts in earnest. "We'll only need three quarters of a cup of the nuts," Moriah said while pouring cider for herself. "I'll have to lightly toast them in the oven then chop some a bit finer. The recipe will make six dozen. I'll send a dozen home with you dear then I'll freeze some for later."

When it appeared that the bowl might contain something close to the needed amount of nuts, Rachel fetched a measuring cup from the house and poured the nuts into it. "Just a few more," she said, holding the cup up and eyeing the three quarter mark.

Armed with a proper measurement of walnuts, the three of us went into the house. The two women prepared the nuts for toasting then collected the recipe's additional ingredients: cake mix, vegetable oil, 1 egg, vanilla extract, and butter. While Rachel added the ingredients to a bowl, Moriah put another stick of wood on her fire. She was quite tall and pencil thin, probably cold on this mid-October day, I thought. Rachel commenting that the old woman had more wrinkles than a raisin wasn't much of a stretch. Her hair, nearly snow white and laced with streaks of pale yellow, had once been that of a flaxen-haired beauty, I thought.

Two of the kitchen's walls were of knotty pine. Cabinets were knotty pine as well. One wall was papered in an olive, floral design. A stone hearth occupied six feet of one wall. The fireplace was open on both sides and let into what I imagined was a living room or din. The kitchen's floor was inlaid tile. Abundant paned windows and recessed lighting gave one a sense of purely natural light. The scent of well seasoned hardwood and pinto beans simmering produced a wonderfully country nuance.

The cookie dough was ready and Moriah said they would only need ten minutes in the oven—two of them that were stacked. When they were done and cooling, she suggested that we take our walk to the cemetery for delivering the flowers. I wanted very much to see the rest of the home. Somewhere within its two thousand square feet or so there must be a library belonging to a most erudite woman. Physics and cosmology are a little much for this newspaper man whose expertise was writing about picnics in the park. But I thought that Dr. Moriah Hawkins was capable of spreading a table with something more than time-worn mathematical equations. How long she and Rachel had known each other I didn't know. One was old and frail of body. Her counterpart seemingly possessed the energy of three women and the beauty to match. But in both women's eyes I saw something that was kindred spirits and beyond.

With cookies baked and cooling on countertops, Moriah found herself a wool shawl, gathered her little bouquet of daisies and the three of us set out for the cemetery. Exiting the house and crossing the porch to three steps that let us onto a well trodden path, we were met by a Hereford cow standing at the picket gate. "Shoo!" Moriah said, reaching for the latch on the gate. The cow swung its white face away and trotted off a few yards. The remaining cattle that Rachel and I had noted when first arriving on the property were grazing near the base of the bluff.

"Whose cattle?" I said.

"Mine," Moriah said, closing the gate behind us. "A local man looks after them for me. He's good to move them around some and not let them overgraze. I won't allow horses in here; they're too hard on pasture, eat it right down to the dirt."

Though the graveyard was pretty much northeast across the meadow, our guide took a sharp right and led us straight for the tree line. "There's a pleasant path through the woods to the cemetery," she said, taking Rachel's arm as we walked. "We won't have to dodge so many cow piles while crossing the pasture," she added. She handed the flowers to me then extracted a tissue from a sweater pocket. She put the tissue to her nose and said, "Cool weather makes my nose run when I get out of doors."

Reaching the tree line and picking our way past a covey of dogwood, now skeletal and barren of foliage, Moriah said, "These trees are gorgeous in the spring. I can see their blossoms in late April or early May from my den window. I so look forward to them. At my age, each sighting may be my last."

"How old are you?" I said, impulsively and wishing, too late, that I hadn't asked.

"Mind your own business, young man," Moriah said, touching my arm then gently taking the flowers once more.

"I learned not to ask that question," Rachel said.

"I'm harmless," Moriah said, bumping me. "And you're still invited to supper."

"Thank you. I'm ever so grateful," I said.

"I love a man with a sense of humor. It's always near the top of lists of what women most look for in men, that is if they're still looking," Moriah said. "I buried two husbands. That's enough," she added.

The path we were upon wound its way just inside the tree line toward the cemetery. With the exception of occasional four legged creatures, I had a sense that the narrow trail was cut by Moriah. Her daily visits when weather permitted kept the forest from reclaiming it entirely. I suspected that her longevity was partially linked to her frequent coming and going through the woods to the graveyard.

Approaching the cemetery's southern border, I was struck by how small it was, home to no more than two dozen markers, I guessed as we broke into its small clearing in the timber. Many of the stones were listing in one direction or another, though none had fallen to the earth. The place wasn't in perpetual care status, but the plots weren't terribly overgrown, partly due to the considerable shade and leaf cover that wouldn't lend itself to proliferating weeds, I thought. A wild grapevine had wrapped itself around one taller gravestone, as though it meant to keep it erect; Mother Nature seeing to those who could no longer look after themselves. Wrought iron fencing had once encompassed the grounds. Only one section of the heavily rusted steel was still standing while its counterparts lay this way and that upon matted grass.

Moriah led us to the middle of the cemetery. Out of respect for those who knew nothing of my presence—*probably*—I stepped around and over the plots as best I could, in so much as I could make out where the dead lay. Moriah and Rachel both noted the care I was taking and glanced at each other but said nothing. We came to a stop in front of four markers. Two of them were pretty much identical in size and fashion; the third and fourth were quite small and obviously that of children, given the dates carved into the granite. I was so fixated on the tiny stones that I only fleetingly noted the names on the two larger ones, marking the spot of Moriah's two husbands, I deduced, though neither of them bore her last name, leading me to further assume that she had retained her maiden name for professional reasons. Whether or not the two men had both died in this part of the country, I couldn't guess. At any rate she had seen to their being interned where she herself intended to spend her own last days.

When Moriah laid the bouquet of flowers before the little stones, I read the inscription:

> *Baby Lilly*
> *Beloved Daughter*
> *Born December 25th, 1963*
> *Died December 25th, 1963*

Little Rosie
3 Years Old
Murdered Christmas Morning

Rachel put an arm around Moriah as we turned to go. "Goodbye, baby girls," the old woman said.

"The other child…" I said somewhat incredulously, looking over my shoulder at the little marker now adorned with a daisy.

"We'll tell you about her another time," Rachel said, cutting short my question, seeming to have anticipated it. She glanced at Moriah who nodded in agreement.

October was showing us shorter days and the sun had already begun its descent behind the tops of the tress to the west when we reached Moriah's house. The cookies had cooled, beans were ready, and the two women mixed cornbread batter. A pot of coffee was brewed. Moriah asked me to add a stick or two of wood to the fire. I sat on the edge of the fireplace hearth with coffee cup in one hand, cookie in the other, and wondered if I ever wanted to return to my own home on Roubidoux Creek.

Four

I woke to the aroma of sausage. I was confused for just a moment when looking at an unfamiliar ceiling. Sitting up in bed, it came to me: I was in one of Moriah's spare bedrooms, of course, for she had invited me and Rachel to spend the night rather than borrow a lantern and find our way back through the forest to the inn. We had stayed much longer than intended. In addition to the pinto beans, cornbread, and pecan pie, our host was marvelous company.

When dessert had been eaten and fresh cups of coffee in hand, we were ushered into Moriah's den where her extraordinary library was housed. I read a fair amount, but I've never been a collector of books. I donate most of the paperbacks I buy to our library; some they add to their collection, others they sell. Strolling in front of Moriah's volumes, a considerable number, even a passing look revealed that her interests were quite rangy, from romance novels to the sciences, some of whose titles I doubted that I could pronounce correctly. Mathematics, physics, theoretical physics, and cosmology in particular occupied most of the shelving, however. The latter subject, cosmology, with its abundant volumes under a good many authors, suggested that this woman thought in very large terms.

Moriah's desk was near the open-ended fireplace that also let into the kitchen. She sat down in a chair near the desk and wrapped a shawl about her slight shoulders. I voluntarily put another stick of wood on the fire. She nodded in appreciation. Rachel and I knew that the visit to the cemetery was still fresh on Moriah's mind when she began speaking: "When I became pregnant with my baby, I was older than what was generally advised in those days. But I was careful about nutrition, exercise, and I was fit. Though my husband and I didn't really care to know if we were going to have a boy or girl, we did settle on names ahead of time. Lilly was our choice for a girl."

Moriah fell silent for long moments. Rachel and I waited. "To say that Lilly being stillborn broke my heart would be an understatement beyond measuring," Moriah continued. "I was utterly crushed and the image of her still little face haunted my days and nights for many years. I sometimes wonder what would have become of me had she opened her eyes for a moment and looked at me before she died. I don't think I could have dealt with it. Our baby's death devastated my husband as well. We clung to each other and wept until we thought we were going to die then and there in each other's arms. He wanted for us to try again, but I thought that I couldn't bear the pain of losing another child, especially like that. And I blamed myself for not being woman enough to bring a healthy child into the world."

"That isn't true, Moriah," Rachel said.

"Well, anyway, that's how I felt back then. I couldn't let the baby go. I started going to séance meetings, behind my husband's back. I thought that he would be terribly angry if he found out. But when I walked into the meeting—oh, the second or third time, guess who was there? He had secretly come and had no idea that I would be there too."

Rachel and I laughed. I suspected that this was not the first time Rachel had heard this story. Moriah joined us in the outrageous serendipity's humor. "We both left before the meeting convened," Moriah continued. "Outside at our cars we laughed, cried, swore, and wondered what in the hell we thought we were *doing*. Neither of us attended another séance. But I still couldn't let the baby go. I began to try and think in more mathematical terms. That's when I read Hugh Everett's paper on quantum mechanics and his theory of many worlds. Everett became awfully obese, drank and smoked too much. Wrestling with such infinite questions may have driven him to all that, I think. Some of his colleagues—even a close friend—distanced themselves from him and his theory of many worlds. In the end, he took up another line of work, at least in terms of trying to make a living at it."

Moriah had a sip of her coffee and pulled the shawl closer about her shoulders.

"Everett was on to something that nobody was willing to even consider being true," she continued. "I think that I myself hadn't Everett's intellect, but I wrestled with many of the same questions and theories. I'm afraid that, at the time, I came up with only one conclusion. Its philosophical simplicity embarrassed some if not most of my colleagues and my own humanistic turn of mind as well."

"And what was that?" I asked.

"That this universe doesn't give up its secrets and treasures to bull-headed morons devoid of imagination and whose mind is already made up about what is and isn't possible. That statement within the body of one of my papers incurred the wrath of much of academia. I meant for them to take it personally, and they did. After I left the university, one of them wrote me an awfully cruel letter and said that I was little more than a mystic and that my papers were most helpful in lighting his fireplace." Moriah laughed softly while reaching for her coffee cup. "I suppose, though, that my calling him and others bull-headed morons was a bit cruel as well. Perhaps I deserved the attack."

Moriah ended her remarkable monologue. I thought that I could have listened to her all day. I was determined to hear more from this woman.

The scent of sausage that had awakened me was added to

gravy and poured over buttermilk biscuits. When breakfast was finished, Rachel and I bid Moriah goodbye for now and set out for the trail that would lead us back through the forest and to the inn. "We must meet again and discuss your book, Evan," Moriah said while she waved us goodbye. Our old friend had sent along a dozen walnut cookies and we munched on one as we walked.

"So, do you think you'd like to hang around for a while?" Rachel said.

"I think so. It's been ages since I've gone anywhere, started to get cabin fever."

"I won't let you get that here," Rachel said, taking my hand once more as we walked. It's a curious phenomenon, it seems to me, female love of going for walks. They and their male counterparts aren't always on the same page, explaining, perhaps, why the girls are more often seen walking with girlfriends.

My mind returned to Rosie's tiny gravestone. "The child buried next to Moriah's baby..." Rachel didn't let me finish my sentence.

"I just love these cookies," she said, finishing hers. She handed me the bag. "Here, take these and keep me out of them." She laughed and brushed crumbs from her fingers. This woman is a master at politely sidestepping subjects she doesn't care to discuss further, I thought. "It's going to be a lovely day," she said. "I'd like to go into town and do some bell ringing for a while. Would you go with me, Evan?"

"Certainly. What town are you talking about?"

"Hawkins Mill."

"Any relationship to Moriah?" I said

"Yes, the mill was in her family. It's a tourist attraction now."

"What's the population?"

"Oh, about 750 or so."

"Donations are good there?" I said.

"Yes. People can't wait for me to come. They think it's so cool that I don't wait for the holidays. They practically want me there *every day*. But I don't want to go overboard, you know."

"Of course not," I said, glancing at a face that was difficult to break away from. We do love a beautiful face, don't we? I thought; a gift to most of us who are homemade soap by comparison. Why folks would want you there every day is no mystery to me, my dear, I mused while having another look at the cashew flecked brown eyes that held mine for just a moment.

"It's kind of tiring, standing there in one place ringing the bell," she continued. "I don't do it for very long, but I love it. You know how these little towns are. People like to stop and talk. I run out of stuff to say after a while, though. So I just keep ringing my bell and smiling until I'm ready to quit and go home. People probably think there's something wrong with me."

"There's *something* wrong with all of us," I said.

Rachel and I stopped at the spring and had a drink, another cookie, then continued on the relatively short distance to the inn. Upon our arrival, we had showers and rested for a while in the great room. That's when I heard another soft knock at the back door off of the kitchen. "I know that sound," Rachel said, getting to her feet. The young girl was standing at the screened door. Rachel went to the door and spoke to her. She came inside. Ushering the girl into the great room, Rachel said, "This is my friend, Evan."

"I'm pleased to meet you," the girl said.

"And I'm pleased to meet you," I returned.

"Hannah wants to practice her singing," Rachel said.

"Angels are *always* practicing their music."

"I'm sure I'll enjoy it."

"Maybe you could help us with your violin," Rachel said.

"I'll try." I went to my room and returned with the instrument.

Rachel sat down at the Baldwin. Hannah took up a spot near the piano. I stood just to the right of Rachel. "Since Christmas isn't far off," Rachel said, "let's do a medley of four carols." She looked to the girl than to me. "Let's warm up with the wonderful old French carol, *Quelle est cette, odeur.* Then *The First Noel, Carol of the Bells*, and end with *How far is it to Bethlehem?* Can you manage those, Evan?" Rachel said, turning to me.

"I'll let the two of you begin then I'll try to join in," I said. "I play by ear, mostly, so maybe I can hang in there decently."

"Hannah does the first carol in French," Rachel said, glancing at me and lifting her eyebrows and smiling.

"Such company I'm in today," I said, clucking my tongue. The girl smiled then gave her attention to Rachel.

"When we get to *Carol of the Bells*, Hannah, you're on your own, a cappella," Rachel said. "I don't know about Evan, but I can't keep up with it on the piano. The timing and cadence is too difficult. Hannah does it brilliantly on her own," Rachel added, looking at me.

"Let the show begin," I said, putting my violin in position.

Rachel did a short intro for the first carol then cued Hannah to begin, which she did, in French: (Author has rendered stanza in English.)

> *Whence is the goodly fragrance flowing,*
> *Stealing our senses all away,*
> *Never the like did come a-blowing,*
> *Shepherds, in flow'ry fields of May,*

Whence is that goodly fragrance flowing,
Stealing our senses all away.

The beauty of the girl's soprano voice cannot be exaggerated. I was so taken by it that I forgot why I was standing there with violin in position. Rachel noted my hiatus and looked up at me from her place at the piano. I came to my senses, drew the bow across the violin's strings and managed a respectable accompaniment. We rolled from the French carol directly into *The First Noel*:

The first Noel, the Angels did say
Was to certain poor shepherds in fields as they lay
In fields where they lay keeping their sheep
On a cold winter's night that was so deep.
Noel, Noel, Noel, Noel

The girl's range was stunning. And on the last Noel, she hit a high C that exploded a light bulb in a floor lamp and left my ears ringing. Rachel ceased her playing, held the girl's eyes for a moment then said, "You know that there's no note that high in this song, Hannah."

"I'm sorry. I forgot," the girl said sheepishly.

Rachel turned slightly to me and whispered, "She's showing off for you." She returned her attention to the girl and said, "If you had any money, dear I'd make you pay for that bulb." Hannah giggled and rolled her eyes to me.

Rachel cleared her throat, shifted her weight on the piano bench then did an intro for *Carol of the Bells* after which she ceased her playing and looked to the girl who launched immediately a cappella into the carol:

Hark! how the bells

Sweet silver bells
All seem to say
Throw cares away
Christmas is here
Bringing good cheer
To young and old
Meek and the bold
Ding, dong, ding, dong
With joyful ring…

It was only by a stroke of luck that the carol was one of my favorites. The violin and I paced the girl in perfect unison, to her obvious delight. Her enormous dark eyes fairly glowed when she saw that I could stay with her. Rachel, silent at the piano, clasped her hands in joy as she leaned back on the piano bench and listened to the performance. "Oh, again, please!" she cried when we had completed the carol. The lovely virtuosa and I launched into the carol again with great confidence in each other. When we had finished, Rachel applauded wildly. Hannah bowed in appreciation.

All but breathless from chasing the carol's notes and the girl's vocal gymnastics, I was glad that we would end the music with something much slower. Rachel took to the piano once more. I drew bow across the violin's strings. The purity and inflection in Hannah's voice brought moisture to my eyes:

How far is it to Bethlehem?
Not very far.
Shall we find the stable room
Lit by a star?
Can we see the little child?
Is He within?
If we lift the wooden latch

May we go in?

Thus we ended our mini concert. Hannah went her way and disappeared into the forest.

Rachel collected her kettle and bell. We exited by the back door and made our way to the garage—more of a shed, I thought—that housed her Jeep. The shed's main door opened in two pieces, each section having to be dragged across rough ground. Inside was an older Cherokee that had obviously seen many a trip through the woods. Its paint, once a navy blue, I thought, was badly faded and oxidized. The radio's staff antenna was broken off halfway down. Chrome was gone from around one headlight. There was little room inside the shed; I waited outside while Rachel started the engine and pulled into the open. Despite its brutalized exterior, the old Jeep idled smoothly and it appeared to have rather new Goodyear Wrangler tires. A flat is the last thing she wanted out in the timber, I figured. I opened a squeaking, moaning door and climbed in. The interior was clean and in excellent condition. Slip covers had been added. The inn's contrast of shabby exterior and impeccable interior crossed my mind as the driver wheeled the Jeep about and headed for the wagon track that had brought my truck here. This is not a woman who thinks a book should be judged by its cover, I thought.

Rachel traversed the jostling route with such speed that I had to cling to the door's armrest with one hand while bracing my feet hard against the floorboard. I didn't care to know what I was in for when we exited the woods and reached pavement. At the moment she was driving like the possessed on their way to an exorcism, as somebody once described a friend's manner while behind the wheel. I've always had a penchant for motion sickness. Just when I began to think it might return, Rachel brought the Jeep to an abrupt stop near the base of the draping willow where the track let out onto the road. "Evan, would you mind getting out and having a peek to see that no cars are coming before I pull out?"

"Certainly," I said, ever so glad that she hadn't opted to simply take her chances and shoot through the willow's tendrils and onto the road. Noting that the coast was clear, I stepped aside while she nosed passed the willow. I jumped back aboard. The Jeep had four speed floor shift and Rachel worked it like a NASCAR driver. She took the serpentine road rather fast as one who was quite familiar with it. "How far is it into town?" I said.

"Six miles." She kept her eyes on the road while speaking and that pleased me. I released my grip on the door's armrest and felt that I had a good chance of making it into town alive.

Reaching our destination, Rachel pulled in front of a small building housing an old time Country Store. "This is where I like to stand. Will you be embarrassed to be with me?" she said, turning to me.

"Not at all," I said.

I'd stand in front of New York's Macy's and peddle handmade hot pads on the 4th of July with this woman, I thought.

"The store has wonderful coffee," she said. "It's brewed in a copper kettle. You get your cup, pull the little handle and out it comes. They grind their own beans like me. Let's have a cup while I'm ringing my bell. It's kind of cool today. The coffee will warm us."

"Sounds good and I'll treat," I said.

"Gladys won't let me pay," Rachel said while reaching for her kettle and bell sitting between us on the bench seat.

With her things in hand, we exited the Jeep and made our way into the store. A woman behind the counter broke into a smile and said, "Hi Rachel."

"Hi to you," Rachel returned as we approached the counter. "Gladys, I'd like you to meet my friend Evan."

"Nice to meet you," Gladys said, quickly assessing me as though I were another of many men seen with Rachel, or one of very few, if any. I found that I would much prefer the latter.

"It's nice to meet you," I said.

"Lovely weather for bell ringing," Gladys said, gazing at Rachel. There was such affection in the woman's eyes that one might have thought they were mother and daughter.

"Yes, we thought it would be perfect," Rachel said, glancing at me. I nodded in agreement.

"Help yourselves to the coffee," Gladys said. We strode a few paces across the room to where the coffee pot and cups were stationed. Rachel handed me the kettle and bell to free up her hands. She poured a cup for each of us. I sampled the smoky brew with pleasure. She twitted her fingers to Gladys as we opened the door and went outside.

We stood in front of the store for a few moments and sipped our coffee. There was a light breeze coming out of the northwest and fallen leaves, still holding to a little of their color, rattled across the street and onto the sidewalk where we stood. Though there was understandably not a great deal of late morning traffic in this town of less than a thousand, I began to sense that something remarkable was afoot when those who were out and about began to slow and look our way. Some made U turns and parked in front of the store. That was Rachel's cue to begin gently ringing her bell. I held her coffee for her.

Gladys, the storekeeper, was the first to arrive, as though she had been standing just inside the door waiting for the sound of the bell. She slipped a bill into the kettle's slot. "God bless you and Merry Christmas," Rachel said.

"And a Merry Christmas to you, dear," Gladys said,

returning to the store.

What began to take place shocked me. People were coming out of the proverbial woodwork. They arrived in cars, trucks—one on a John Deere tractor—scooters and bicycles. They came from a drugstore, out of alleyways, gas station, barber shop and beauty salon. One old woman who appeared to be stove up with arthritis was all but running to where Rachel and I stood. "Good morning, honey," the old woman said in a crackling voice. "I was so afraid I might miss you this time," she added while depositing change into the kettle.

"God bless you and Merry Christmas, Mabel" Rachel said.

"Thank you and the same to you my dear."

Donor after donor after donor found their way to her kettle while Rachel gently rang the little bell. At one point they were crowding about her like betters at a horse track, some reaching past and over others to stuff their money into the kettle's slot, as though they feared the race might begin before they could place their wagers. I held her cup so that she could have a couple sips of her coffee. She sighed, rolled her eyes to me and said "Thank You." I was struck so dumb that I could scarcely stop staring at her. With the exception of an occasional stranger, she knew all of their names. There was not a hint of anything perfunctory in her greeting to each one.

What I was seeing was nothing close to the usual site surrounding that charity drive we all have come to know. Oh, to have this woman on every corner! Here was a virtual stampede to get money to the kettle.

I thought that the donors would never quit coming, but there was just enough break for us to make a run for it. "They can catch me next time," Rachel said as we drove away.

We rode in silence for a few moments then I said, "I've never seen anything like that. You must have some sort of spell over those people."

"They just love giving."

"How is it that the media hasn't showed up?"

"They did, once, and got such a cold reception they left. Nobody would talk to them. After a while, though, some were sneaking around in the forest with cameras. Gunshots were heard. They've not been back."

"Who did the shooting?" I asked. Rachel only shrugged her shoulders.

"What's going on here is nobody's business but ours. Anyway, if you open the door to them once, they won't leave you alone."

"Well, I'm an old newspaper man and I'm asking too many questions. It's none of my business anyway," I said.

"It will be in time, if you stay around for a while," she said, reaching and taking my hand. "Moriah and I want to make sure you can handle what we'll tell you."

I'm already hearing voices, I thought.

"I need to go home and check on my place eventually," I said.

"I'd like to go with you, Evan," Rachel said, rounding a curve then slowing dramatically when seeing a deer on the shoulder. "They'll jump right out in front of you sometimes," she said then resuming her speed when the deer turned and bolted back into the timber.

"One more question," I said, still holding her hand.

"I'm listening."

"What do you see in me? I'm just an average looking guy."

"When I first met you on the overlook, I heard a gentle kindness in your voice. It's very soothing to me. I see truth in your eyes. And I think you're a good looking man, Evan."

"What you see is what you get. I'm just Evan Van Clevin any way you cut it."

"That rhymes," Rachel said with a smile playing at the corners of her mouth.

"Yes, I think you noted that once before."

"And you have a sense of humor, too," she said as we came to the spot at the willow where we would turn onto the wagon track. "Moriah saw that," she added while the Jeep brushed past the willow tendrils.

"An interesting woman," I said. "I'd like to see her again."

"I'm sure you will."

"Just one more question. I promise that it's the last, for a while," I said.

"Let's hear it."

"Are you sure you're not wearing any perfume?"

"I'm sure," she said, laughing. "I do require a bath or shower like everyone else, though."

"Imagine that."

Five

Rachel and I spent the better part of the week just hanging out at the inn. I'm no carpenter, but I offered to help with fixing a thing or two, a little paint here and there. She politely declined, saying she was afraid that if the place got to looking too respectable people would start inquiring into lodgings. She had a point. We did venture off the grounds to visit a pecan grove and returned with enough nuts to keep us busy shelling for a number of hours, on and off. She would make some pies and freeze them for the holidays, she said.

My new friend's taste in music knew both ends of the pendulum: bluegrass to classical. We listened to some Rhonda Vincent (Missouri girl and unprecedented six consecutive International Bluegrass Association Female Vocalist of the Year) then I found a CD from the truck's glove compartment and we cracked and picked pecans to Horowitz' piano and laughed at how cosmopolitan we had become.

During these hours and days with this woman I began to see a saliently transparent personality. In her unassuming way she could be as sophisticated as a New York debutante, yet down to earth as a can of pork and beans. Who could count the bitter tears of men who had lost such a prize? Sorry, guys. Evan Van Clevin is suited up and standing on the sidelines with helmet on. If I take the field and she calls my number in the huddle and unloads a bomb for the end zone, I'll blow by you so fast you'll leave the game with pneumonia! I'll go up in triple coverage and come down with the ball! And with both feet in bounds!

On a crisp Saturday morning that left heavy frost on every pumpkin in Rachel's part of the Mark Twain National Forest, we loaded into my truck and picked up State Highways 19 and 68, north to St. James. There, we would connect with Interstate 44 west to Waynesville and Roubidoux Creek.

Since leaving Kansas City and the newspaper and moving to Pulaski County, my journalistic pen lay rather quiet. But writers are habitual if not compulsive observers and analysts of their surroundings and those who people it. The resiliency of Ozarkers, especially those living in the more densely forested areas, intrigued me more and more. I found them to be masters at finding ways to make a living in such remote and often brutally steep and rocky landscapes. I wondered how many of the early settlers—mostly European—lived past mid-life while trying to clear enough timber and rock to plant a little corn. Of course timber could be sold; stave mills and harvesting of white oak, used exclusively for wine barrels, was once quite prominent. My own father cut staves for fifty cents a day in the early going of the last century.

Pulaski County is famous for its truck patches from which come some of the best melons to be found anywhere. Soil composition was no doubt a factor in the proliferation, but I suspect that less acreage needed played a role in mom and pop's decision making. Hill folks were experts at formulating moonshine, but marketing it could land one in the pen at Jefferson City; best to enjoy recreational nips out of a Mason jar at home.

Leaving the hard stuff, one can always milk a few cows, I thought after crossing the Current River and observing a small herd of Guernsey making their way laboriously along a narrow path toward a milk barn where their bulging utters would be relieved. Vapor drifted away from their mouths and noses on this very cool morning while they chewed their cud and trailed politely behind each other as if they knew—and they did—that their personal stall would be waiting. "Aren't they gorgeous animals?" Rachel said. "They're very docile, too," she added while watching the cows pick their way across a rocky draw and up a steep embankment. "My family owned some of them long ago. They produce something like 16,000 to 18,000 pounds of milk a year and on 20 to 30% less feed than most other dairy cows. They do well on pasture. And their milk is some of the best in the world, very rich in cream. They're expensive animals, though."

"With that kind of production I'm not surprised," I said.

We were nearing Interstate 44 where we would head west to Waynesville. "Have you had a pot of chili yet this fall?" I said.

"No, but I'd love some."

"Let's have an early lunch when we get to Waynesville," I said. "There's a really good home owned café on the square. After lunch we'll do a little grocery shopping. I'll put the chili on to slow cook then we can do some exploring along Roubidoux Creek."

"Wonderful," Rachel said. "I haven't been anywhere for sooo long. This will be like a vacation for me."

We rolled into Waynesville a little ahead of the lunch hour, beating what is often a line of folks waiting to get into the café on the square. We enjoyed chicken and dumplings, sweet iced tea, and apple strudel for dessert.

Driving to a grocery store, we gathered ingredients needed for the pot of chili; Rachel suggested pitching a single bay leaf into the mix. We found a bottle of cabernet to enjoy by a fire later in the evening.

My cabin on the creek was as I had left it; it had neither burned nor been burglarized. We unloaded our groceries and duffels. I gave my guest a tour of the log house, which didn't take long, being only 1500 square feet. She was immediately taken by the simple charm and its seclusion. Both gregarious and private person, Rachel, I thought. Her inn is an absolute hideaway into which a discernable road no longer leeds. Yet her warmth while chatting with those who donated to her kettle in Hawkins Mill was remarkable.

After putting on our pot of chili we set out upstream along the banks of Roubidoux Creek. It was fun to wade in warmer temperatures, I told my guest. She rolled up her jeans to the knee and began wadding the moderately swift but shallow current anyway. "Our sneakers will dry by the fire," she said, coaxing me to follow her, which I did somewhat reluctantly and with a shiver. Fortunately, the Roubidoux has a great many gravel bars affording intermittent relief from the cold water. Minnows and grayfish had not yet taken to deeper pools providing shelter when ice begins to form, for they fled before us while we sloshed forward.

Having made our way a hundred yards or so upstream, we rounded a turn and decided to sit a while on an outcropping of limestone that protruded onto a gravel bar. The finely washed stones were strewn with halved mussel shells, pried apart by skilled and powerful paws. It was mid-afternoon and the sun was finding its way through the timber and warming the rock upon which we sat. The yellowing leaves of towering cottonwood danced under a slight breeze, sending the sun's rays to us in shimmering shafts of light. "What a beautiful spot," Rachel said, taking my hand and leaning against me gently. "It's very romantic, don't you think, Evan?"

"Yes."

"I wonder how many young lovers have sat here," Rachel said, pressing against me a bit closer.

"I couldn't count that far," I said.

After some moments of silence, Rachel said, "It's been so long since I've been kissed. I can hardly remember the last time."

She turned to me slightly, my cue, I thought. "I'd be happy to end that drought," I said, looking into her brown eyes.

"Please do." We were by now sitting so close that I had no need to draw her nearer. I put my lips upon hers and the rock upon which we sat began to rise and rotate like a merry-go-round. She moaned softly and put one hand on my face as our lips parted. "Another one," she whispered. I was still levitating, but my lips found hers once more.

We lay back upon the rock and let the sun warm our faces. Then, "Would you spend the holidays with me at the inn, Evan?"

"Yes," I said, drawing a deep breath and releasing it slowly.

"We'll have Thanksgiving dinner with Moriah."

"Turkey, dressing, and pumpkin pie?"

"All the trimmings," she said, closing her eyes once more to the sun. "I'm taking her one of my hams, so we'll have that too." She was quiet for some moments. Then, "You're a good kisser, Evan. Can I have more sometime?"

"All you want," I said. "You rang my bell, dear." She laughed softly and squeezed my hand.

We noted that the sun had descended considerably from its point when we first set out along the Roubidoux. The temperature was cooling rapidly and wadding back down the creek toward home wasn't nearly so inviting. But our sneakers were already wet and going downstream would be easier.

Upon reaching the cabin, we hurriedly removed our wet shoes and donned warm, dry socks. I got a fire going in the hearth then made a pot of coffee. My guest stirred the chili and said that it was coming along nicely. I put on a Horowitz CD and we sat on the edge of the hearth and sipped our coffee. Rachel said that she thought it must have been quite a culture shock for me, moving from Kansas City to this remote place. I agreed. When cabin fever set in I ventured into Waynesville to mix with a few fellow humans.

Our supper was ready by five o'clock. I found a box of saltines and we ladled up the chili and took our seats by the hearth once more. "This is excellent chili," Rachel said, blowing across a spoon full then depositing it into her mouth.

"I think the bay leaf adds a little something," I said, sampling from my own bowl.

"Yes. I learned it from Moriah. She's a fabulous cook. You're in for a treat Thanksgiving. I can assure you of that."

"Physics and cosmology is a little deep for me," I said, stirring my chili then filling the spoon again. "But I would have loved to sit in on one of her classes."

"They filled up quickly, I understand," Rachel said. "She was invited to deliver a series of lectures at Oxford on Parallel Universe theory and her views on what might be *out there*—or, as close to us as our hands and feet, she sometimes suggests. British newspapers said you couldn't have gotten a seat in the lecture hall with a gun."

"I think I might have sneaked in the night before with a sleeping bag," I said, chuckling and taking up my coffee cup.

"I suspect some had the same idea."

We enjoyed our chili in some moments of silence. I very much wanted to pursue the subject at hand but had a sense from Rachel's body language that she would rather not. I believed that something profound was afoot at Hawkins Mill. A secret so closely guarded as to send gunshots ringing through the forest. Once a newspaper man always a newspaper man. But whatever was going on down there wasn't a story that would be broken by me; betraying a friend has never been on my list of things to do. And, too—friendship not withstanding— the snub nosed 38 that she carried in the *pseudo* Salvation Army kettle wasn't to be taken lightly. I had no doubt that she knew how to use it. My years on the *Star* hadn't won me a

Pulitzer for investigative reporting. I'm not the greatest sleuth; distaste for privacy invasion tends to hobble a need to dig into someone else's business. But a gut feeling was telling me that there was more to Rachel's bell ringing than raising money for neglected and abused children, worthy as that is.

I had no cheese to go with our wine. But cheesecake, possibly the next best thing, was in my freezer and I thawed it in the microwave. I added a couple sticks of hickory to the fire. Rachel and I moved from the edge of the hearth and sat on the plush carpeting, cradling our saucer of dessert in our laps and testing the wine. It went quite well with cheesecake, we agreed, and wondered if we might be the inventors of such a combination.

The two of us seemed to be intent on getting closer to the floor and each other. When the cheesecake had been eaten, I found a couple of couch pillows for our heads. Our fire had burned to a perfect state, a nice bed of glowing embers beneath the freshly added sticks of wood. "I think the fire is all the light we need, don't you, Evan?" Rachel said, rising on one elbow and reaching for her wine glass.

Agreeing, I got up and turned off the lights. Returning to my friend on the floor in front of the fire, I took another sip from my wine and set the glass on the hearth. Rachel sampled her wine once more then set it beside mine. She pulled me close as she lay back, so close that I could feel her heart beating. "I'm glad you got lost on the overlook, Evan," she said, putting one hand on the back of my head then pressing her lips to mine.

"Yes, a wonderful stroke of misfortune," I whispered when our lips parted.

That great October moon that had depressed me my first night on the overlook was making its way into the darkness once more. Through my cabin's one bay window we could see it rising slowly above Roubidoux Creek. Rachel stroked my head with one hand while her other began to unbutton her blouse.

✳

No more than a stone's throw upstream from the little cedar log cabin where two lovers were doing what the moon was created for, a raccoon sat at the water's edge and foraged about in search of muscles. It raised its dripping paw from the stream and turned a masked face toward the cabin and the cry of a human voice: "Evaaan! Yes! Yes! Oh God! Evan baaabyyy!"

The night grew still. The raccoon resumed its search for crustacean delicacies while the Roubidoux flowed quietly past. The fat creature turned and waddled a few feet upstream, turned and looked back toward the cabin again then continued on its nocturnal way. It shook its head once, possibly to sling water droplets from its whiskers while moving unhurriedly along the pebbled banks of the Roubidoux.

Six

I'm not the first average looking guy to fantasize about making love to a beautiful woman. Though I'm decently secure in my own skin, most of the time, that is until I hit the big Five 0, Rachel made me feel like I'm more than I am. "Screaming orgasm" jokes at local pub happy hour are familiar. There's even a drink named after it. But by God it's no joke when the creature you are loving cuts loose with *Yes! Yes!* and damn near dislocates your hips with her clutching. Oh, such sweet pain! It's beyond ego trip. The irony is that she so absorbed me I forgot about her beauty. She could have been as plain as pasta with no sauce. What ran through my skyrocketing senses was that here is female through and through.

I might say that I saw stars just before entering the calm eye of our hurricane; perhaps it had passed over me and I was being swept into the other side. That would have been a comforting cliché, seeing stars, in place of the image that rather shook me: Rachel was standing at the gravesite of Moriah Hawkins' stillborn baby, and little Rosie, murdered on Christmas day, whose death I had yet to learn any details. Autumn leaves, as gorgeous as I've ever seen them, drifted lazily from the trees and came to rest at Rachel's feet. The kettle was in her left hand while her right hand slowly rang the bell. Her brown eyes, disturbingly haunting as anything out of Sleepy Hollow, were fixed on me, as if beckoning me to cross over.

Steinbeck once said that making love to a woman purifies a man. At any rate, the first time changes the chemistry of a relationship. You look at each other differently the next morning, if she hasn't gotten up and left in the middle of the night. One cannot imagine anything more intimate than lying naked beside each other. A man can never feel more accepted than when a woman welcomes him into her most private domain. I was so fulfilled that I wanted to thank her for having me. I didn't, lest my fragile heart become too transparent, though a wise woman once said that women respect men for their strength; they love them for their vulnerability.

Eating hotcakes and sausage with one hand is relatively simple. A good thing, for my lover and I scarcely turned loose of each other's hand during breakfast. For the life of us we couldn't stop sighing; so much so that we began to laugh at ourselves. "I think I just turned seventeen last night," she said.

"Yes, and I'm wondering if I'll need a new pair of shoes for the prom," I said.

After placing an order for propane to see the cabin through the holidays, and collecting a few more clothes for my extended absence, we set out for the inn. Light rain, little more than mist, had begun to fall. I set the truck's wipers on intermittent. I figured that we were on the leading edge of the front; occasional gusts of wind whipped falling leaves across the road. The sodden leaves stuck to the truck's windshield like flattened leaches before the wipers swept them away.

A day and night can sometimes accelerate the progress of a relationship between a man and woman, if not always in the most desirable direction. Rachel and I couldn't continue our breakfast hand holding, for I needed both hands on the wheel. But she had found her way to the middle of the seat; we sat as close as a couple of teenagers cruising on a Friday night date.

Nearing the Current River where we had seen the Guernsey making their way toward a milk barn, we saw them once more, only coming in the opposite direction. Utters, having been relieved of their rich milk, swung not so heavily as the cows picked their way in single file along the same familiar path that would lead them to pasture. "I'd like to have some of their fresh milk to take home," Rachel said as she watched the cows' progress. "I have a separator for the cream," she added.

"Let's go ask," I said, slowing and watching for a drive that would lead us to the barn. Seeing no entrance as such, I eased the truck onto the road's shoulder. Light rain had ended for now and we opted to walk the cow's path to the barn where we found a man and woman hosing down milking equipment. "Hello," I said.

"Good morning," a man in bib overalls said, turning to us as we stood in a doorway. A woman cleaning equipment a few stalls away smiled and brushed hair from her eyes.

"We saw your wonderful Guernsey cows," Rachel began while we strolled on into the barn. "My family used to own some of them," she added as we came to a stop before the man. The woman, whom we assumed was his wife, joined us. "I'm Rachel Mountjoy, this is my friend Evan Van Clevin," my partner said, extending her hand to the woman. The woman smiled, cut to me when I extended a hand to her husband. I was thankful that neither of them commented on my sing song name.

"Wouldn't have anything else," the man said, releasing my hand and taking Rachel's. They introduced themselves as Joe and Martha Milton. "Where you folks from?" the man said.

"I'm from up at Waynesville, on Roubidoux Creek," I said, joining the conversation. "We're heading to Rachel's place near Hawkins Mill for the holidays," I added.

"We've heard that there's a woman down there who does the Salvation Army thing, you know, kettle, little bell, out in front of a store, even when it's not Christmas time," Martha said. She seemed fixated on Rachel's face. Then, "People up this way say she's very beautiful."

"I've heard about her ... could I possibly buy a little of the milk?" Rachel said, changing the subject rather abruptly. She smiled and lifted her eyebrows in anticipation. "I have a separator for the cream. It would be so good with pumpkin pie at Thanksgiving."

"It's fabulous," Martha said almost absently while continuing to gaze at Rachel. "You won't find anything like it in a store."

"I'll *give* you some," Joe Milton said. "How much would you like?"

"Half gallon?"

"You should have more than that if you're going to separate … how about a couple of gallons?" Joe said. He cut briefly to his wife who nodded and smiled in agreement then turned and strode to a cabinet and found a pair of gallon jugs. He washed them out and filled them from one of the stainless steel tanks into which the morning milking had been deposited.

"Thank you *so much*," Rachel said. "I'm going to take some of the cream to Moriah," she added, looking at me.

"Would that be Moriah Hawkins?" Joe Milton said.

"Yes," Rachel returned.

"How is she?"

"Old as these hills but still going strong," Rachel said. "We're having Thanksgiving with her," she added.

The two of us chatted with Joe and Martha Milton for a few minutes then excused ourselves so that they could return to their chores. Reaching the doorway, we turned at the sound of Martha's voice. She strode quickly to where we stood. She withdrew a ten dollar bill from the front pocket of her jeans then said, "If you happen to see that woman, you know, ringing her little bell in front of the store, please put this in her kettle for us."

"I will," Rachel said.

As we left the barn we heard Joe Milton say, "God bless you, Rachel Mountjoy. And Happy Holidays to you both."

"And to you as well," I said, turning to the couple as we

walked away, each of us carrying a gallon of gift from the Guernseys and Miltons. I glanced at my friend then took her free hand and said, "Your beauty and good deeds precede you." She squeezed my hand but said nothing.

Light rain had returned. We quickened our pace to the truck, avoiding the cow path as it began to look a bit slippery; any vestige of grass had long since been trampled out of existence by the cows' twice daily trek to and from the barn.

The storm system moved through quickly and by the time we reached the inn the sun was shining. Rain had preceded a cold front, for we found upon exiting the truck that temperatures were plummeting. We hurriedly unloaded our baggage and two gallons of milk. Rachel put on coffee and I built a fire at her request. It was nearing the lunch hour and she fixed the two of us chicken salad sandwiches and promised pecan pie, regretting that the Guernsey cream hadn't yet been separated. We'd have to settle for Swiss Miss.

While we savored our pie, I thought that Rachel looked preoccupied. "That there's no lane or sign for the inn isn't the only reason people don't come here anymore, Evan," she said. My pie was finished and I set the saucer down on the counter and waited for what I sensed was going to be an important revelation about this increasingly mysterious place.

"A year after my husband was killed in the car crash, another tragedy happened, here, at the inn. I was still open for business then. It was Christmas Eve when a woman and a young girl pulled into the drive. They came to the desk and the woman said she and her daughter would like to stay here for a few days during the holidays. The woman looked to be in her late thirties; the child was three, I learned later. She was a gorgeous little red head with big green eyes. I gave them a lovely room on the second floor across from the balcony."

Rachel was silent for a few moments, had a thoughtful bit

of her coffee then continued. "What was the child's name?" I said.

"Rosie."

The name on the gravestone raced across my mind and I felt the hair rise slightly on my forearms.

"I had no other guests at the time," Rachel continued. "I told the woman that supper would be served at six o'clock. When the two of them came down and took a place at the table, I could smell liquor on the woman's breath. The child said not a word during the entire meal. She was attracted to the Christmas tree in the great room, a ten-footer that I always decorate with great care. I tried to coax conversation from her, you know, excited about Christmas, Santa Clause, I wonder if we'll get any snow, the usual banal stuff. I finally gave up and let them eat alone."

Rachel grew silent once more, took up her coffee cup but declined anymore and set the cup back down, as though she had gotten a bad taste in her mouth. She drew a deep breath and released it slowly, looking at me as if she were pondering whether or not to continue the story. She did:

"At three o'clock in the morning I heard the woman raise her voice to the girl. I could hear the child crying. At first I thought I should go to their door, but decided to mind my own business, at least for the time being. I lay in bed listening. I was about to drift off to sleep when I heard their door slam and something hit the downstairs floor. I got out of bed and ran into the foyer. I found the child lying unconscious below the balcony."

"My God," I said.

"I dropped to my knees beside the girl and lifted her head in my hand, frantically trying to get a response. I could feel no pulse. I was out of my mind with fear. I first ran upstairs to their room. The door was locked. I ran back downstairs and called 911. It was a while before police and ambulance arrived. I regretted having let the lane to the inn grow over. But they managed to get through.

The child's mother had chained the door. The police broke it down and found the woman hanging from a bed sheet in a closet. An autopsy was performed on the girl and her neck had been broken by the fall. They found, too, that she had old fractures on her arm and one of her legs. It appeared that she had been abused for much if not all of her three years before being thrown to her death."

"One of the great tragedies of our time," I said. "It's estimated that 5 to 6 children die each day in this country from neglect and abuse."

Rachel reached for a tissue and dabbed at her eyes then said, "They were the last guests this inn had. It was all over the media, of course. I couldn't blame anyone for not wanting to stay here. And the tragedy happening in the wee hours of Christmas morning made it all the worse."

"How in the name of God did you cope with it, being here alone?" I said.

"I had Moriah. I went and stayed with her for a while. I didn't know if I could come back here. But it was my home and I had nowhere else to go. Moriah told me not to run from it. It would follow me. I couldn't sleep after returning here. But I knew that Moriah was right. I had to stick it out and let time do its thing. I decided that I would never operate the inn again. My income was gone. I sold off all but a hundred acres, as I told you earlier, and invested the money so that I would have something to live on. I wasn't getting past what happened here very well. Some people from town would come now and then to check on me and that helped, them not thinking that the inn was cursed. But I knew that I had to occupy myself with something. That's when I decided to find a way to raise money and donate it to organizations that help neglected and abused children."

"That's where the kettle and bell came in," I said.

"Yes. I told Moriah what I was going to do. She thought it a wonderful idea and said that she wanted to go with me the first time. She said that she hadn't had a chance to put money in a kettle for ages!"

"What time of year was it?" I asked.

"February. It was snowing and the forest was so beautiful. I picked Moriah up and we laughed on the way to town, wondering what people would think about seeing us out there, me with the kettle and ringing the bell—in February. I said that I thought I would stand in front of the little store, if Gladys didn't mind. When we reached town, Moriah and I went into the store and got a cup of coffee. I had my kettle and bell with me. I asked Gladys if she would mind if I stood in front of the store and rang the bell."

I couldn't help but chuckle at this point.

"She didn't quite know what to say," Rachel continued. "Finally she said, 'Well, of course, dear, but the holidays are past. It's February.' I know, I said, but I've decided to do something to help neglected and abused children. By the look on her face, I think Gladys was worried that I wasn't getting over the tragedy very well, and she was right."

"I think it would have gotten to me," I said.

"Moriah and I finished our coffee and went out in front of the store. Here goes, I said. 'Ring that *bell*, girl,' Moriah said, standing beside me."

"What a woman!" I said.

"It was still snowing," Rachel continued, "and there weren't many people out. Some that drove by did a double take when they saw me and Moriah standing in front of the store. They turned around and drove past again then came back and parked when they recognized the two of us ... everybody knows everybody in these little towns. The first person to come up to us was Wilbur Higgins, a local farmer. He said hello to both of us then put $20 in the kettle. God bless you, Wilbur, and Merry Christmas, I said. His eyes moistened then he gave me and Moriah a hug and returned to his pickup. He watched us for the longest time. I think he was trying to figure out what was going on with me. People began showing up, just a few at first, then more and more. I think they started making phone calls. Moriah and I had never gotten so many hugs and well wishes in our lives!"

"How long did you stay?" I said.

"About an hour, I think. Moriah was getting cold. We were heading for my Jeep when we saw a young girl standing across the street. She had on a parka with fur around the hood. She looked like she was 12 or 13 years old. She had a very lovely, mature face with large, somber eyes. Blonde hair protruded from beneath the parka's hood. She just stood there staring at us. Moriah thought maybe she needed a ride somewhere. I swung the Jeep around and pulled alongside the girl. Do you need a ride somewhere, honey? I said. She shook her head slowly form side to side then said, 'I heard the little bell.' Then she vanished."

"She ran away?" I said.

"No. She simply disappeared—gone, instantly."

"What are you saying?"

"I'm saying that she was there then she was gone, without a trace, not even tracks in the snow," Rachel said.

"Could you have been hallucinating?" I said, tipping my head with tongue in cheek.

"If I was, so was Moriah, because she saw the girl too."

"Have you seen her since?" I said.

"Yes. And so have you, Evan."

"Hannah?"

"Yes. The next time I saw her she came to my back door. She wouldn't come inside. I asked her name and she said Hannah. I asked how old she is and she didn't know. I asked where she lived and she said everywhere."

"Are we talking ghosts here?" I said.

"Do ghosts wear parkas with fur around its hood?"

"I've never heard of it. Then again I've never seen a ghost," I said.

"I'm surprised that you're not pooh poohing this, Evan."

"I do have something of a mystic turn of mind. *The Abyss* and *Field of Dreams* are two of my favorite movies. Besides, I've heard a voice."

I decided to tell her the most recent, lest she think me borderline psychotic.

"What do you mean?" Rachel said.

"When I was leaving home to drive to Springfield to buy my new truck, I heard a voice when I crossed Roubidoux Creek."

"What did it say?"

"*A voice is heard in Ramah, weeping and great mourning, Rachel weeping for her children and she would not be comforted because they are no more.*"

"That's from the Bible, Evan."

"I know. I looked it up. I thought that I might be getting a little wacky, spending too much time alone. I heard the voice again in a restaurant in Springfield."

"This is weird."

"I think that my getting lost on the overlook wasn't an accident. I've been summoned to this place and it's starting to get a little scary," I said.

"Are you going to leave?"

"Not on your life, lady."

Seven

Thanksgiving morning found a dusting of fresh snow on the floor of the Mark Twain National Forest, Rachel Mountjoy's part of it anyway. We rose at daylight—from the same bed ... my feet were the warmest they had been in years, and had a light breakfast of oatmeal. Rachel wanted to be at Moriah's early to help with dinner preparations. She fetched a pecan and pumpkin pie from the freezer and a pint of the Guernsey's cream from a refrigerator. We put on coats and made our way to the smokehouse where a ham was selected and added to the things destined for Thanksgiving dinner.

This would not be a day for walking to our old friend's place, of course, and light snow was still falling. The Jeep was four-wheel-drive and it would easily navigate the trail that Rachel and I had taken on my first visit to Moriah's. We opted, however, to take the long way around, passing through Hawkins Mill then on to a more proper road to Moriah's. We packed a change of clothes and toiletries in case the storm became major and we needed to spend a night away from the inn.

Main Street in Hawkins Mill was deserted this Thanksgiving morning, with one exception: a man in topcoat and stocking cap sat on a bench in front of the Country Store where Rachel and I stood while she rang her bell. Two small duffels sat on the bench beside him. Upon seeing us nearing the store, the fellow rose to his feet rather stiffly and flagged us. Rachel pulled to the curb and rolled her window down. The stranger was an older man. He came to the curb and spoke: "Thank God!" he said in a heavily German accent. "I've been waiting here since daylight hoping someone would come by."

"Has your car broken down?" Rachel said.

"No, I've hitchhiked from Springfield," the man said. He seemed quite exhausted and removed his stocking cap. He ran trembling hands through a shock of hair white as the snow that was falling. Though there was fatigue in his face, pale blue eyes spoke of intelligence behind them. His German did a curious twist on the word Springfield. I wasn't sure what he had said. Neither was Rachel.

"Where did you say you hitchhiked from?" Rachel said.

"Springfield," the man said. He seemed to sense our difficulty in understanding him and struggled to pronounce the name of the city more clearly.

"Where are you trying to go?" Rachel said.

"I must see Dr. Moriah Hawkins," the fellow said. "I have come from Heidelberg, Germany. A very difficult trip, I'm afraid. My luggage was lost. I escaped with only these two bags that I carried on the plane. I meant to rent a car but my credit card was not accepted."

"We're on our way to Moriah's for Thanksgiving," Rachel said. "Get in. We'll be happy to take you there."

"Oh my heavens! What a stroke of luck!"

The man opened the back door of the Jeep, set his duffels inside then climbed in. He closed the door, took a deep breath and released it with a rush then introduced himself as Rachel pulled away from the curb. "I'm Wolfgang von Kepler," he said, extending his right hand over the back seat. Rachel and I shook his hand and introduced ourselves.

"Is Moriah expecting you?" Rachel said.

"I'm afraid not. I had no phone number for her and I left Germany on awfully short notice. All I could learn is that she lives in America, Missouri, somewhere in the Mark Twain National Forest and near a town named after her family."

There was remarkable urgency in the man's voice. Rachel

and I glanced at each other but declined to question the fellow regarding his need to see Moriah. "You're certainly invited to have dinner with us," Rachel said.

"Oh, I shall very much enjoy one of your American Thanksgiving dinners," von Kepler said. "I've had nothing but a tuna sandwich from a vending machine last evening."

"Poor man," Rachel said. "Moriah is a wonderful cook."

We rode in silence for a few moments then I said, "So, Mr. von Kepler, what do you do in Heidelberg?"

"I'm at the university ... physics, cosmology, those sorts of things."

I cut to Rachel and she blinked a couple times then glanced at me. "How did you come to know Moriah, if you don't mind me asking?" I said, looking over my shoulder at the gentleman.

"We've never met. I know of her writings, of course. I shall apologize to the good woman for dropping in like this, but something quite extraordinary has occurred and I must speak with her about it." With that von Kepler turned to one of his duffels, unzipped it and withdrew a red kettle and little bell. He held them up for us to see. "I'm sure you've seen these in your country," he said.

Rachel looked into the rearview mirror and all but lost control of the Jeep. She swerved onto the gravel shoulder, sending rock and snow flying before she regained the pavement. "Forgive me for distracting you," von Kepler said, rising from the floor of the Jeep where he had been thrown. He clankingly retrieved the kettle and bell.

"Where did you get those?" Rachel said, trying to sound calm.

"I found them at my door the morning before I booked a flight to America. I thought that perhaps some of my students were playing a prank. I was about to return them to The Salvation Army. I put on my coat and hat then rang the little bell before leaving my house. That's when I had a visitor. She was standing just outside my door when I opened it."

We reached our turnoff and Rachel swung the Jeep onto a one lane gravel road that would lead us into the valley where Moriah's house stood, I assumed. So taken by the dense timber, now flocked with snow, von Kepler left off with his story and said, "So like my Germany, your Mark Twain National Forest."

After what I judged to be a mile drive through the forest, we broke into the clearing where Moriah's house stood. Her half dozen Herford cattle were bunched around a gigantic roll of hay. Vapor rose from their nostrils in the frigid air as they raised their heads and continued chewing while watching us drive slowly past.

We parked at the rear of Moriah's house. Noting our arrival, she wiped a swath of steam from her kitchen window and peered out at us. We unloaded the Jeep and made our way through an inch of fresh snow to the back door. She opened to us. As we stepped inside, her eyes were fixed on the old fellow. He quickly removed his stocking cap, as though he were somehow remiss in the woman's presence. Moriah's eyes widened a bit as she gazed upon her visitor. "Dr. von Kepler?" she said in her crackling voice.

"Yes, my dear," von Kepler said, extending a hand to Moriah. Then, "Have we met and I've forgotten?"

"No, not that I recall," Moriah said. "But I recognized you from a photo on the back of one of your books in my library. What brings you to America and my home?" Moriah said, releasing von Kepler's hand.

"Something most extraordinary," von Kepler said. "But first, if I could rest for just a bit. I've had a very long and difficult journey. Perhaps I could lie down for a little while."

"Of course," Moriah said. Then, "Rachel, would you be good enough to show Dr. von Kepler to the guest room?"

"Certainly," Rachel said. von Kepler picked up his two bags and followed Rachel out of the kitchen.

When Rachel returned, Moriah said, "Where on earth did you find him?"

"He was sitting in front of the store when we drove into town," Rachel said. "The poor man flagged us down. He had flown into Springfield but was unable to rent a car. He hitchhiked to Hawkins Mill. He said that he had to see you. It sounded quite urgent."

"He's absolutely exhausted," Moriah said.

"Wait until you see what he has in one of his duffels," I said.

"What is it?" Moriah said.

"We'll let him show you," Rachel said, glancing at me.

"Would you mind to bring in a little more wood, Evan?" Moriah said as she and Rachel began to get busy in the kitchen.

After collecting firewood, I was given a fresh cup of coffee and a slice of fruitcake. I sat on the hearth in the kitchen and wondered what Moriah's reaction would be when von Kepler presented his kettle and bell and told of the young visitor at his door. If she had no answer, there would be a theory, no doubt. I had one of my own, a theory, but I would suspend it, for now, in the presence of more erudite minds. Beyond theory, however, I believed that Hawkins Mill townsfolk suspected that something extraordinary was afoot in their little village. One thing was for certain, assuming that Rachel was telling the truth regarding the girl's vanishing act: paranormal was in our midst. Why so few people had witnessed it was probably no great mystery. If anything is universally agreed upon in things supernatural, it's that there are no wholesale appearances. Those ghostly subjects are quite picky about whom they choose to reveal themselves.

I had begun to come to a conclusion: the shots fired in the

forest to dissuade meddling media were from Rachel's 38. She knew that if this story got out, Hawkins Mill would be inundated with reporters. I couldn't imagine, though, that she and Moriah could be so naïve as to think their secret could be kept forever. Media would suspend judgment, pretty much, until the facts were in. But otherwise, why cast one's pearls before swine only to have them ridiculed and rationalized to death?

At two o'clock, announcement came from the kitchen that Thanksgiving dinner would be on the table in fifteen minutes; time to wake Dr. von Kepler. I went to the guest room and found him up and combing his air. I could still see some jet lag in his face, but he looked considerably less fatigued than when Rachel and I first spotted him sitting in front of the store. "Let's wait until after dinner before I share my story with Moriah," von Kepler said.

"Excellent idea," I said as we headed for the door. "Turkey and ghosts don't go well together."

"I rather think that this is more than ghosts," von Kepler said, touching my arm then falling silent while we neared the dining room.

I myself am no atheist, a tad agnostic, perhaps. I can't speak for Rachel or Moriah. But we were all three rather surprised when von Kepler asked if he might return grace. We respectfully bowed our heads:

"Heavenly Father, we give you thanks this day for the goodness and plenty that is spread before us. Bless the hands that have prepared it. May we not forget those who have little or nothing on such a day—"

His voice trailed off in what seemed only a hiatus. I glanced up fleetingly to see if his eyes were still closed. They were and I closed mine and bowed my head once more when he continued:

"We sense of late that we are being spoken to. Forgive our slowness of mind in your presence. We shall try with all our might to understand and to act. Amen."

When I raised my head and opened my eyes, Moriah had beaten me to it. Her attention was locked onto von Kepler. She broke from him and invited us to start passing food around the table. After we had supplied our plates and sampled a little of each, Moriah said, "I must say, Wolfgang, that I'm most anxious to learn what it is that has brought you to my home in such urgency. And to what do I owe this pleasure of meeting a man who is arguably the finest living cosmologist on earth."

"You're much too generous, my dear," von Kepler said, taking fork and knife to a slice of ham. "It is I who has come to sit and *your* feet. When we're finished enjoying this wonderful meal, I have something to share with you. Then I shall insist on hearing an uncanny response so characteristic of one of yours I heard in Berlin in the summer of 1960," von Kepler said, casting a smile at Moriah.

Rachel and I were torn between enjoying the meal and getting back to what von Kepler had in one of his duffels. Our eyes kept meeting. Moriah noted it and probably thought that we were falling in love. She might have been right. At any rate, we were standing together in a nexus of unspeakable dimension ... *dimension* ... yes, that in fact may be the operative word here. *Another* dimension would be more accurate, perhaps. I could see anticipation in Moriah's eyes as well. We were all determined to do the meal justice and we patiently gave it its due. When time for pie and coffee rolled around, however, I felt my pulse begin to quicken; soon we would be gathered in Moriah's library and attempting to solve a mystery for which we had no precedent or historical, empirical tools. Our only edge would be two of the finest theoretical physics minds in the world. This would require more: a jump from what is sometimes called the classical universe to something beyond, not yet indentified, the stuff of science fiction. But science fiction resulted in taking us to the moon. And recently I've read that one of our ingenious snoopers is believed to have left our beloved Milky Way, having taken something like 30 years to do so at breakneck, ludicrous speed. Science—even folks on the street—long for new frontiers. It may very well be staring us in the face here on our own little planet at Hawkins Mill.

With the meal finished and fresh cups of coffee in hand, the four of us retired to Moriah's study. Dr. von Kepler set his coffee cup down and went directly to the guest room and returned with the duffel that had occupied most of my thoughts during dinner in spite of Rachel's succulent ham retrieved from her smokehouse. Moriah was understandably curious about what was in the duffel and von Kepler didn't keep her waiting. When he withdrew the kettle and bell, Moriah's coffee cup, on its way to her mouth, came to a halt. She set it back on an end table near her.

Though this was only my second meeting with Moriah, it was the first time that I had seen confusion on her face. Moriah cut to Rachel who was of little help with only a shrug of her shoulders. "Forgive me for being nosy, Wolfgang, but what are you doing with those, other than having joined The Salvation Army?" Moriah said. Rachel and I chuckled; von Kepler didn't.

"I found these most iconic little jewels at my door a few mornings ago," von Kepler said, beginning to reiterate the truncated story that Rachel and I had heard. "I took them inside, thinking that some of my students were pulling a prank. I rang the little bell then put on my coat and hat and was about to return the things to a Salvation Army office I knew to be not far from where I live. When I opened the door, a young woman was standing there. She looked to be in her early teens, possibly. She had a remarkably lovely face, large somber eyes as richly brown as wet walnut shells. She was wearing a gorgeous parka with what appeared to be real wolf fur bordering the hood. The hood was not on her head and glorious blonde hair looked as if she had been caught in a great wind."

I shot a look at Rachel and she clandestinely mouthed the words, Hannah. I nodded slightly in concurrence.

Dr. von Kepler continued: "I asked the girl if I could help her with something. She shook her head. I asked if she knew where the kettle and bell came from and she said yes. It was the first time that I had heard her speak. Her voice matched the maturity in her eyes, though I still thought that she was quite young. I asked her name and she said Hannah. I asked where she lived and she said everywhere. I had a follow up question but she cut me off and said, 'I heard the little bell. You must go to America and talk with my friend Moriah at Hawkins Mill. Please take the kettle and bell with you.' With that she simply vanished before I could ask her friend's last name. In academia, Moriah Hawkins is a household name. Two and two was an easy equation. I decided that the town must have been named after your family, Moriah. I went on the Internet and found you in Missouri's Mark Twain National Forest."

"Rachel has a kettle and bell," Moriah said, "though she came by hers in a different way. She painted hers pink. She too has met the young woman that appeared at your door in Heidelberg. Evan has met her as well."

With that Moriah deferred to Rachel who turned to von Kepler and took up the story more or less from the beginning: "Five years ago there was a tragedy at the inn where I live. A woman who had taken lodgings became drunk and through her three-year-old daughter over the inn's second floor banister. I found the child dead. The mother hanged herself from a bed sheet in a closet."

"Good God!" von Kepler said.

"I closed the inn, though I remained there," Rachel continued. "I had to find a way to get my mind off of what had happened. "I found a kettle in a flea market and had a local metal worker make a lid for it. I painted the kettle pink. I found the little bell in a gift shop. I began going into Hawkins Mill to raise money for neglected and abused children. Moriah went with me on my first trip. We stood in front of the Country Store where you were sitting. We were met with a wonderful response. When we were done for that outing, we saw a young girl standing near the curb across the street. I drove over and asked if she needed a ride somewhere. She simply shook her head. She said that she had heard the little bell."

"How was she dressed and what did she look like?" von Kepler said.

"Precisely as you described your visitor," Rachel said.

Moriah hadn't contributed much to the dialog. I glanced at her and thought I could see wheels turning in her brain. Rachel continued: "The authorities had a difficult time locating next of kin for the mother and child. An aunt came forward, finally. She said that she was so poor she couldn't manage taking proper care of the remains of both. I asked if I might be allowed to bury the child's remains. She said yes. I buried the little girl next to Moriah's baby in a cemetery not far from here."

"What was the child's name?" von Kepler asked.

"Rosie. Two little flowers—Rosie and Lilly—lying side by side," Rachel said. "Moriah takes them a bouquet almost every day."

"What a tragic but moving story," von Kepler said.

We all looked to Moriah. She took a thoughtful sip from her coffee cup then began with what was a jarring explanation: "Every good theory must make a prediction. If the prediction doesn't come to pass, the theory must be abandoned. Forty years ago I predicted that there is within the vortex, if you will, of a parallel universe the remains of sub-atomic particles poised to make an appearance in the world as we know it. That prediction was made after I left the University of Chicago, thank goodness. For shortly thereafter I was savaged by a number of colleagues, not there, but in other institutions."

Moriah became silent, sampled her coffee once more and asked me to put another log on the fire. I hurriedly did so, fearing that I might miss some of what she had to say next. She waited until I had stoked the fire and regained my seat next to Rachel.

"The verbal flogging I received from certain quarters of academia wasn't brought on entirely by my theory and prediction; calling some of my colleagues unbelieving morons devoid of imagination, or something like that, contributed to it, I'm afraid," Moriah said, chuckling and taking up her coffee cup once more. "They know, as I do, that the universe, what we can observe of it, is expanding; evolving, perhaps we could say. Our knowledge sometimes is one step forward, two backward. But knowledge of all that we see is evolving nevertheless. I think that the *mind*, if I may be allowed to be so familiar, at the heart of this universe does not reveal its secrets to those who will not believe a thing possible; indeed, they will not so much as seek evidence."

"How are we now more believing than in the past, Moriah?" von Kepler asked.

This is getting good, I thought, taking up my own coffee cup.

"I don't know that we are," Moriah said.

I thought that she had suddenly flung us back to square one. I was mistaken.

"When I cast my bread upon cold cosmic waters, I wasn't looking for a theological response from *out there* in the darkness," Moriah continued. "My theory and prediction was based on Peter Higgs' boson subatomic particle theory that there is such a particle responsible for drawing dark matter—of which most of the universe is comprised—into a mass. It is sometimes called the God particle, much to the displeasure of most scientists. And I rather doubt that Peter Higgs would buy into my theory that his boson particle is the parent, if you will, of living entities within a parallel universe."

"Forgive my slowness to grasp where it is you are going with this, Moriah," von Kepler said. He picked up his kettle and bell and said, "I can't imagine, however, that any of this is connected to the venerable Salvation Army."

We all laughed, though we weren't quite sure if von Kepler's remark was meant to be satirical. We were satisfied that our finding humor hadn't offended him.

"I rather think that the kettle and bell which we have all have come to know and love has nothing to do, directly, with what is transpiring. What I do think, however, is that when Rachel rang her bell for the first time on Main Street, she inadvertently struck a nerve on some unspeakably secret stage. Perhaps it—or, they were waiting in the wings for just such an unpretentious cue. The kettle and bell do symbolize caring."

I had yet to utter a word during these conversations. I feared sounding banal in the midst of such intellect. What the hell … damn the torpedoes: "Are we talking about God, here?" I ventured.

"I don't know," Moriah said. "I think that the word God is simply a name we've employed for the purpose of trying to explain what is, at the moment, unexplainable. Out of obvious language necessity we have to give everything a name. How else could we make reference? I for one can't imagine that the genetic code found in every living thing did not emerge from an intelligent entity at its beginning. Evolve, yes, but a *beginning* nonetheless."

"I think that we're losing our way here," von Kepler said, chuckling. We all laughed and agreed.

"I have a down to earth question," Rachel said, evoking more laughter. "If our Hannah has in fact leapt into our world from another dimension, where did she get that lovely parka with the fur trim?"

"It is a beautiful thing, isn't it?" Moriah said, smiling as though somehow refreshed by this terrestrial diversion. "Forgive me for hogging this conversation," she continued, "but I think that Hannah is what we may call an envoy, forward observer. It's clear—to those of us who have witnessed her ability to materialize then dematerialize before our eyes—that she is not of this world. She knows that, of course. Simply wearing a white sheet would not do. Someone may have given her the coat. Perhaps she came by a bit of money, somehow, and bought it."

We all laughed.

"I wonder if she could get me a parka like that." Rachel added, bringing on more laughter. Then, "Hannah asked me to make her a monk's robe. You must see it, Moriah. I made it out of Merino wool. It's just beautiful."

"Interestingly, Hannah means *grace*, or *favor* in Hebrew," Moriah said. "Hannah is about to grace or favor us with something most important."

"She certainly graced me and Evan with her singing," Rachel said.

"She sings like an absolute angel," I said. "I've never heard anything like it from a child her age—an adult, for that matter."

"Singing like an angel may be more than a metaphor," Moriah said.

"Why has she come?" von Kepler asked.

"I don't know," Moriah said. "But I think she is waiting to

see if we can be trusted."

"Trusted in what way?" Rachel said.

"I don't know that either, as yet. I think that at the proper time we'll know what is going to be asked of us. I don't think that she has come to just hang out."

A prolonged silence gripped the room. I thought that we were somehow closing in on the essence of Hannah. Rachel was sensing something from me. She turned to me and said softly, "Tell them about the voice you heard."

"I should tell you about something I experienced—*heard*, perhaps I should say," I began. "It was in the middle of October of this year. I was at my home on Roubidoux Creek up in Pulaski County. I had decided to drive to Springfield and trade my aging SUV in on a new pickup. As I was crossing the creek near my cabin, I heard a voice. I thought that maybe the radio was on. It wasn't. Or maybe somebody was talking somewhere near along the creek's bank. There was no one."

"What did the voice say?" von Kepler asked.

A voice is heard in Ramah, weeping and great mourning, Rachel weeping for her children and refusing to be comforted because they are no more.

Moriah looked at Rachel then von Kepler. "I suppose that the next question is if what I heard was the proverbial small, still voice inside my head. The answer is no," I said. "It was a clear, level voice that seemed to surround me, almost like I was sitting in a theater with Dolby sound. But it was soft, as if meant for only me to hear."

"What did you think when learning Rachel's name when first meeting her at the overlook the night you became lost?" Moriah said.

"I was a bit shaken, to say the least."

"Did you hear it again after leaving your home?" von Kepler said.

"Yes, in the restaurant of the hotel where I meant to spend the night while my new truck was being serviced. I overturned my coffee cup."

"Evan has written and published a book with an intriguing title," Moriah said, turning to von Kepler. *You May or May Not be Crazy.* Is that the book's correct title, Evan?"

"Yes."

"What is it about?" von Kepler said.

"Hearing voices," I said, evoking chuckles. "The central thesis is that most schizophrenics hear voices, but not all people who hear voices are necessarily schizophrenic."

"Most interesting," von Kepler said. Moriah nodded in agreement.

"Do you believe in a spirit world?" Moriah asked.

"Sometimes," I said. "I have a somewhat mystic turn of mind."

"Do you have medical training?" von Kepler said.

"No. I wrote a community column for a newspaper. The book has sold pretty well. I think I just got lucky and hit on a nerve. We're all feeling a little crazy these days."

"I agree," Rachel said to everyone's agreement.

Moriah turned her attention to a nearby window then said, "I see that it's quit snowing, for now, and it hasn't gotten too awfully deep, maybe a couple of inches. I have some lovely silk flowers that I'd like to take to the cemetery. It's a rather short walk. Would you all mind going along with me?"

"Certainly not," von Kepler said. We all agreed.

"When we get back, we'll have some hot cider to warm us," Moriah said.

Moriah went to a closet and collected her silk flowers. She found boots, gloves, donned a coat and wool scarf which she wrapped about her head and throat then joined the rest of us who were ready and waiting at the door. Rachel and I walked on either side of her, an arm entwined with hers to see that she didn't fall. von Kepler trailed closely behind. There were in fact no more than a couple of inches of snow on the ground and the going was easy enough. Contrary to my first visit to the old graveyard, we cut diagonally across the pasture this time and made straight for our destination. One of Moriah's cows had delivered a calf and it followed us at a short distance. Its mother wasn't far behind. von Kepler's wingtips weren't suitable for this trip, but the three of us walking ahead of him broke the trail adequately to keep the snow out of his shoe tops.

The trees encompassing the cemetery were flocked with snow, some of which showered down lightly in intermittent wind that found its way through the forest. We drew the collars of our coats more firmly about us to keep the snow from going down our necks as we found our way to Moriah's family plot. Little more than an inch of powdery snow lay on the crest of each of the gravestones marking where her two husbands lay. I bent over and brushed snow from the two almost ground level markers where Lilly and Rosie rested. Moriah separated her flowers, dividing them equally then laid them upon the graves. "Goodbye girls," she said softly then turned to go. The rest of us followed in silence. It struck me as odd that though her two husbands got a flower, she had no parting words for them; they had had many more years upon this earth for such farewells.

When we reached the warmth of Moriah's home, she and Rachel prepared the cider. I stoked the fire and we all stood near it to warm our backsides. With our cups of hot cider in hand, we continued to stand near the fireplace. It seemed that we had run out of much else to say. Dr. von Kepler broke the silence: "So, what are we to make of all this? What are we to do, if anything?"

"I think that we must wait," Moriah said. "If you aren't pressed to return to Germany," she added, looking to von Kepler, "I want you to take my guest room."

"Actually, I'm on a sabbatical," von Kepler said.

"Good," Moriah said. "I think that we're going to need all the brain power we can muster, and soon."

Eight

Dr. von Kepler made arrangements for staying in America until the New Year. Rachel offered to share in lodging him, but Moriah insisted on keeping the professor at her home. She was enjoying his company very much. And he was quite a good cook, introducing his host to some fine German dishes.

We had not seen Hannah since before Thanksgiving. On a Saturday morning in the second week of December, however, she appeared at Rachel's back door while we were having breakfast. Rachel asked her to come inside and she did so. She stood silently before us for long moments then said, "I heard Mr. von Kepler ring the little bell. He's a nice man. He can help ... sometime."

"In what way?" Rachel said.

I could see a shift in the girl's dark eyes. I thought that she was going to answer the question. She didn't and took a different tack entirely. "Missymammy thinks me and some of my friends should have a concert in front of the little store on Christmas Eve. Do you think they would let us?"

Rachel looked stunned. The hair had begun to stand on the back of my neck, again, something of a lifelong, feline thing that I often find annoying. Not this time. "Yes, I—I think that would be wonderful," Rachel said, shooting a look at me. I nodded in agreement. "Who is Missymammy?" Rachel added.

"Just Missymammy," Hannah said. "She takes care of us. She made me the pretty coat that I wanted."

"Does she sew?" Rachel said, glancing at her sewing machine.

"Sort of, I guess," Hannah said, twittering the fingers of both hands as though she were sprinkling stardust.

"Where does Missymammy live?" I asked, venturing into

the dialog.

"Everywhere," Hannah said.

The girl seemed to have said all she wanted to say and was about to leave. In an effort to somehow extend this conversation, Rachel said, "Would you like some breakfast?"

"I don't eat," Hannah said. "I'm nuclear powered." She giggled delightfully.

"Well, you do have a certain glow," Rachel said.

Hannah giggled again then ran her hands admiringly down the monk's robe. "I'm having so much fun going around in the forest like a monk," she said, turning and heading for the door.

"How will we know about the concert's time?" Rachel said.

"When it's dark, we will be there," Hannah said. "Please make sure that Moriah and Mr. von Kepler come."

"I will," Rachel said.

When the girl had gone, Rachel drew a deep breath and blew out her cheeks, practically dropping into her chair. "That's the most I've ever heard her talk," Rachel said. "I think we're getting close, to what, I don't know."

"Have you offered her something to eat before?" I said.

"Yes, a couple of times. She only shook her head."

"Nuclear powered ... Missymammy! We've got to share this with Moriah and von Kepler," I said, finishing my toast. Rachel practically crammed her last slice of toast into her mouth. We collected our coats and headed out the door. "Can we take the shortcut with the Jeep?" I said.

"Yes."

When Rachel had pulled the Jeep from the shed, I climbed in. "Fasten your seatbelt," she said, "this route really isn't for vehicles but I've driven it before." I was glad that I hadn't brought along coffee. I could feel all four wheels pulling hard in the snow cover. I turned and looked out the back window; the Jeep was slinging snow and acorns for five feet behind us.

We mounted a rise in the terrain so fast that we became airborne before landing on the other side. "Sorry, I meant to slow down before we hit that," Rachel said, apologetically.

"No problem," I said, checking to see if my seatbelt was properly secured. "Would you happen to have a helmet I could wear?" I said with tongue in cheek.

Rachel laughed but kept her eyes on the trail ahead. "Believe it or not, I've never hit a tree in all the years I've been doing this."

"That's comforting."

We came to a sliding stop just short of the fence surrounding Moriah's home. We got out and strode to the back of the house. Moriah and von Kepler were finishing breakfast. Rachel knocked on the door. Moriah rose from her chair and opened to us. We must have had rather intense looks on our faces, for Moriah said, "What's happened?"

"We had a visit from Hannah this morning," Rachel said as the two of us took seats at the table."

"And what did she have to say?" Moriah said, shooting a look at von Kepler.

"She said that Missymammy thinks she and some of her friends should have a concert Christmas Eve in front of the store."

"Who is Missymammy?" Moriah said.

"Rachel asked the same question," I said. 'Just Missymammy, she takes care of us. She made me the pretty coat that I wanted,' she said. I asked her where Missymammy lives. 'Everywhere,' she said."

"Most interesting," von Kepler said.

"There's more," Rachel said. "A couple of times since Hannah first appeared to me, I asked if she wanted something to eat. She would only shake her head. I asked her again this time, hoping to keep her a while longer and learn more. She said that she doesn't eat and that she's nuclear powered. There's been some sort of break through with her, and I think Dr. von Kepler's arrival has something to do with it," Rachel ended.

"We've been discussing these developments almost day and night," Moriah said, cutting to von Kepler. "We've come to a conclusion that Hannah, Missymammy, now—whoever on this earth or heaven *she* is—have been meticulously assembling accomplices. I think that a Christmas Eve concert is only a prelude to something much bigger."

"I agree," von Kepler said. Then, turning directly to Rachel, he said, "Have you ever touched the girl, hand on a shoulder, something like that?"

"No," Rachel said. "I started to take her hand once and she backed away."

"We have a theory about that," Moriah said, glancing once more at von Kepler who nodded in concurrence, "and Hannah saying that she is nuclear powered supports it. I believe that what we are seeing is a three dimensional image of the girl. You would grasp nothing, should you attempt to touch her."

"She isn't real?" Rachel said.

"Oh, she's real alright," von Kepler put in. "But not in a sense that we're accustomed to. She's got switches, buttons—if you will—that can turn her on and off in terms of whom she chooses to let see her. She can be cloaked in any garment she chooses. And she's probably capable of traveling at the speed of light."

"How in the name of everything rational could something like this be happening and here in our little corner of the universe?" Rachel said.

"Assuming that we have been uniquely chosen," Moriah said, "it may be because of our willingness to believe. I took an awful lot of flack in one of my papers many years ago regarding unwillingness of many—too many—in the scientific world to believe in even the possibility of a parallel universe, let alone there being living entities within it."

"Surely the four of us aren't the only believers on this earth who could be chosen to take part in whatever it is that we're to take part in," Rachel said.

"I agree," I said, feeling like a knot on the trunk of an oak tree in the midst of all this intellectual bantering. "There's an old adage in the media which says, in effect, that every story is local. At least that's where they must begin. There's another media adage: every story must have a face. No face, no story. We've certainly got that with Hannah; lovely child. Her blonde hair and haunting dark eyes are breathtaking."

"The cosmos has sent an egg down its Fallopian tube for us to fertilize," Moriah said. "I think that has occurred. It has attached itself to the lining of our universe and waits to be born, if I may use such a metaphor."

"What a brilliant way to put it!" von Kepler said.

"And may I add that your impeccable credentials in the scientific world—Moriah and Dr. von Kepler—has probably played a major role in our being chosen," I said.

"I don't like that word, *chosen*," Rachel said, chuckling. "I prefer to choose, not to be chosen."

"Well, it appears that Missymammy has chosen us all, and that may be that," Moriah said. "At any rate, I wonder what we're to expect with the concert," she added.

"Carols in a cappella, I suppose," Rachel said.

"I wonder if they'll have a conductor," Moriah said.

"I guess we'll find out," von Kepler said. "Maybe it will be Missymammy," he added, evoking chuckles from us all.

"Well, I better get into town and start doing some bell ringing and spread the word," Rachel said. "I don't know what I'll tell people when they ask who the singers are and where they are from?"

"Just tell them you found a band of angels who love to sing," I said.

"That may be more literally true than we think," Moriah said.

Rachel and I left Moriah's home and returned to the inn by the same route through the forest, slower this time, I was happy to note. We were going to collect her kettle and bell and drive into town for some bell ringing and begin announcing plans for the concert in front of the store on Christmas Eve. How many would come out in the cold would be anybody's guess. It was my guess, however, that folks would pack Main Street in every direction. I suspected, too, that they would not be disappointed. My greatest *fear*: the presence of media. None of us had so much as a clue regarding who or how many singers would arrive, let alone what they may look like. I hoped that they didn't simply *appear* or *materialize* right before everyone's eyes. Missymammy had better have something clever up her three dimensional sleeve for her choir's entrance that will pass for normal. Otherwise forget the music. Bring on the EMS units to attend to those who have fainted or dropped dead.

The snow had ended by the time we left Moriah's. Rachel and I reached Hawkins Mill at noon. Entering the store, we were greeted by Gladys. She invited us to help ourselves to the coffee. Rachel took this opportunity to announce plans for a Christmas Eve concert and asked if it would be alright to stage it in front of the store. Gladys had no problem with it. She hoped, though, that it wouldn't be too cold or snowing heavily. "Who will be providing the music?" she asked, looking first at Rachel then to me. I deferred to my partner.

"A girl in the area came to me and asked if she and some of her friends could sing carols on Christmas Eve," Rachel said. "It sounded like they might have quite a bit of experience, you know, singing different places," she added.

"Do I know the girl?" Gladys said.

"I—I don't think so," Rachel said. "She lives way out in the forest."

Rachel was struggling. I sensed that she would have difficulty fielding many questions regarding the singers, more precisely where they were from and their ages. "Nothing like hearing children singing Christmas music," I said somewhat lamely. Gladys seemed satisfied and said that she was looking forward to it and would spread the word. We told her the concert would begin at dark.

We left the store and Rachel began to ring her bell. It wasn't long before we started to get some customers. In addition to blessing each donor and wishing them a Merry Christmas, Rachel informed them that there was to be a concert in front of the store beginning at dark on Christmas Eve. A children's choir, she said, only guessing that the singers would in fact be exclusively children.

Word had gotten around about the visitor from Germany. Folks were curious and Rachel said that Dr. von Kepler was a fellow scientist. He had come to America from Heidelberg, Germany to discuss some theories with Moriah. Nobody cared to ask about the nature of such theories, seeing that there were no scientists among them, it appeared. And one must be careful about broaching questions that can't be responded to intelligently. Better to smile and nod then let it go at that.

My worst fear, that media would show up at the concert and sense something unusual about the choir members, came to pass early, if only in part. A gentleman wearing a navy blue top coat stepped up to Rachel's kettle and inserted a crisp twenty dollar bill. "God bless you and Merry Christmas," Rachel said.

"And a Merry Christmas to you, Rachel Mountjoy," the

fellow said. He stepped to one side to allow donors to put their money in the kettle. "Allow me to introduce myself," the man said. "I'm Charles Newton from *The New York Times.*"

"What do you want?" Rachel said. She removed the kettle's lid, retrieved the man's twenty dollar bill and returned it. The fellow reluctantly took his money, looking as though his feelings had been hurt. A newspaper man myself, if retired, I thought Rachel had acted brashly. During my years with *The Kansas City Star* I was no stranger to rudeness on occasion when I thought it was unwarranted. Perhaps rudeness is never warranted, for that matter.

"I've never seen you before," Rachel added. "How is that you know my name?"

"My family and I were in Branson taking in some Christmas shows five years ago. The tragedy of the child's death at your inn was in the news. A terrible thing," the man said.

"Yes, it was a great tragedy," Rachel said with less edge in her voice. "What brings you to Hawkins Mill?" she added.

"I was wondering if the inn has reopened and if you have a vacancy."

"Yes, there is a vacancy, but I will never reopen the inn."

"The child who was thrown to her death, her name was Rosie, is that right?" the reporter said.

Rachel cut briefly to a couple of donors, smiled, gave them her usual benediction then returned her attention to the *Times* reporter. "Yes, her name was Rosie." Then, "If you don't mind, Mr. Newton, I would like to be more respectful of those who are contributing to my kettle and give them full attention."

"Of course," the man said. He turned to enter the store then stopped and said, "I understand that you're going to have a Christmas Eve concert here on Main Street, a children's choir. Is that right?"

"Yes," Rachel said, an edge returning to her voice.

When the reporter had gone into the store, Rachel turned to me and said, "I was afraid of this."

"It could be innocent enough," I said.

"Reporters are never innocent," she returned, "with the exception of you, Evan," she added, touching my arm.

Rachel wanted to remain a while longer and resume getting the word out regarding the concert. She had suspended that announcement in the presence of the reporter who, as it turned out, had learned of it independently. I had no intention of alarming Rachel further, but I suspected that the man was on to more than just our plans for the concert. He had somehow learned of Dr. von Kepler's arrival in Hawkins Mill, I thought. In the elite world of cosmology, Moriah Hawkins and Wolfgang von Kepler are names as familiar as McDonald's and Walmart. When Rachel and I returned to the inn, I was going to fire up my laptop and see if I could find a little bio on Charles Newton, especially his particular area of interest.

Rachel nudged me, turning my attention across the street. Hannah was standing near the curb, obviously knowing that passersby were impervious to her presence simply because they could not see her. She was clad in her monk's robe. She smiled and waved then vanished. That instantaneous departure took my breath, for I had never seen her leave us in that way. She had always walked off into the forest until out of sight. Hannah's visit, albeit brief, made us less anxious about the arrival of Charles Newton and the *New York Times*. For all we knew, given what was looking more and more like a systematic calling of cast to Hawkins Mill, Mr. Charles Newton was Missymammy's—or, Hannah's latest member. Perhaps the two were working in tandem. I doubted, though, that Newton had been graced with the privilege of *seeing* Hannah. Had that been the case, he probably would have broken the story by now, swamping Hawkins Mill with media.

When Rachel had tired of ringing her bell and felt that she had gotten out enough word regarding the concert, we returned to the inn and got both of our laptops up and running. Rachel was the first to find some bio on our *New York Times* reporter. "Whoa!" she said, turning to me. "Last year he won a Pulitzer for a story he did."

"What was it about?" I asked, ceasing my own search.

"*Child Abuse in America: An Unpaved Road to Social Ruin.*"

"That certainly explains his interest in the tragedy here at the inn," I said.

"There's more," Rachel said, scrolling on the page she had pulled up on her laptop. "He published a Bestseller three years ago."

"What's the title?" I said.

"*The World Next Door*," Rachel said. She was silent for long moments, apparently reading something. She glanced at me but said nothing then continued to read. Then, "It's a layman's guide to parallel universe theory."

"Bingo," I said.

"Listen to this *New York Times* review," she said: 'Charles Newton's book is a look into one of the most fascinating hypotheses of our time. Newton is no astrophysicist, cosmologist, or a man who is, by his own admission, not even very good at math; a certain irony, given his last name. But he has done his homework. Though the book is mercifully lean on equations, at times one gets the feeling that the author has sat at the feet of none other than Stephen Hawking. That said, I was stunned at the author's belief—even prediction—that we are nearing a threshold upon which we shall view things unspeakably exciting.'"

"I wonder if Moriah or von Kepler has read the book," I said.

"Possibly, but I doubt that those two consider him exactly a heavyweight in their field."

"Assuming that the man isn't clairvoyant, I can't imagine how he could possibly have gotten wind of Hannah's presence," I said.

"I think he's fishing. But he's got some good bait," Rachel said.

"What do you mean?"

"The shots in the forest that I told you about…"

"Driving off reporters?"

"Yes. Those shots were from my 38. One of the reporters saw my face in the moonlight."

"Do you think it was Newton who saw you?"

"Possibly. I emptied the gun over their heads, but it probably scared the crap out of them. It would me. They may have thought I was some moonshiner protecting my still," Rachel said, chuckling.

"It won't be me who breaks this story," I said, "but I think it's only a matter of time before it gets out."

"I agree. You know what I think, Evan?"

"What."

"I think that is precisely someone's goal, Hannah, Missymammy—whoever or *whatever* is fueling this. There's a point that is going to be driven home when the time is right."

"I hope we don't wear out our welcome, but I think we need to get back down to Moriah's and talk with her and von Kepler regarding our visitor from New York," I said.

"Those two aren't likely to tire of this subject," Rachel said, as we shut down our laptops. "Moriah was just getting started when we were there last. I could see wheels turning in that remarkable brain. If she lives long enough, that woman is headed for Stockholm and a Nobel Prize."

Nine

Just when the four of us esoteric sleuths thought that we had the sibylline ingredients pretty much in our ghostly pot and simmering nicely, it came to a boil and blew the lid off in the form of a phone call to the inn. Rachel answered. The conversation was short. "Evan and I will be there in a few minutes," Rachel said, turning to me. "That was Gladys at the store. She says there is a Professor Charlotte Conrad from St. Louis University who needs to see me as soon as possible."

"Do you know what it's about?" I said.

"Do I know what anything is about these days?" Rachel said. We found coats and made our way to the Jeep. Fifteen minutes later we pulled into a parking spot in front of the store. Inside, we saw Gladys standing behind the counter. She motioned to a corner table where a woman was sitting alone. She noted our arrival and guessed that we were who she was looking for.

Rachel and I strode to the woman's table. She rose from her chair to greet us. "I'm Charlotte Conrad from St. Louis University," she said, taking Rachel's hand first then mine. I found that her hand was trembling. "Thank you for coming," she said.

The woman appeared to be in her early forties. Shoulder length brunette hair was laced with grey. Her eyes were pale blue behind wire rimmed glasses. She was wearing a navy blue pea coat which she had unbuttoned, exposing a paisley sweater of greens and burgundy. She had a half empty cup of the store's coffee sitting before her. Rachel turned to me and said, "Evan, would you mind to get us some coffee?"

"Certainly not," I said. I asked our visitor if I could warm hers and she agreed.

Returning with the coffee, Rachel thanked me then waited for the woman to begin the conversation. "I'm in the music department at St. Louis University," she began, clasping and unclasping her hands before her on the table somewhat nervously. "I teach music theory, piano, voice, and direct choral and ensemble."

"You're a very busy woman," I said.

She seemed to become distracted, as though she had forgotten what she was about to say next. She gazed at me and Rachel alternately then said, "Early this morning I had put on sweats and was about to leave my home for my usual jog. When I opened the door, I found these." She turned in her chair and reached into a Macy's shopping bag sitting beside her on the floor and extracted a red kettle and little brass bell.

"Here we go again," Rachel whispered, glancing at me.

"I didn't know what on earth to think," the woman said. "I donate things to The Salvation Army on occasion. But I've never heard of them giving these to people." She looked at the kettle and bell now sitting on the table. "I sat down in a chair and lifted the lid to the kettle to see if there was anything inside," she continued. "It was empty. I rang the little bell. That's when I heard a knock on my door. When I opened, a young woman was standing there. She was wearing a beautiful parka with what looked like wolf or coyote fur bordering the hood. She was quite lovely with a fabulous head of blonde hair and enormous dark eyes."

Rachel and I glanced at each other then returned our attention to the woman.

"I asked her if I could help her with something," the woman continued. "She smiled and said, 'I heard the little bell.' I asked her if she had left the kettle and bell and she said yes. I asked her why and she said, 'You must go to Hawkins Mill and talk to my friend Rachel Mountjoy. We will need your help.' I asked her name and she said 'Hannah.' I asked her where she lived and she said 'everywhere.' Then she just vanished," the woman said with a breaking voice. "I don't mean that she ran away. She *disappeared*." The woman's eyes misted over and she cast about the store, as though she were looking for the girl. "Finding this place was difficult, and I almost turned back. But I had to find out if what I saw and heard was real," she said, getting a tissue from her coat pocket and dabbing at her nose.

"It's real. And if you're crazy, so are we because we've met the young woman, Hannah," Rachel said. "I have a kettle and bell, too, though I came by mine differently. A man from Heidelberg, Germany—whom you must meet—has them as well. He received his in the same way that you did."

"This is so weird," the woman said, dabbing at her nose once more then stuffing the tissue into her coat pocket.

"Do you need to return to St. Louis tonight?" Rachel asked.

"I have a class tomorrow afternoon."

"We'd like for you to meet two people," Rachel continued. "They aren't far from here. You can leave your car in front of the store, it'll be safe. You can ride with us. Bring the kettle and bell."

With Professor Charlotte Conrad aboard, Rachel backed the Jeep away from the curb and wheeled it about in the middle of the street. "It's a short drive through the forest," Rachel said, turning slightly and looking at her passenger in the back seat.

"Whom am I to meet?" Charlotte asked.

"Moriah Hawkins and Dr. Wolfgang von Kepler," Rachel said.

"Would that be Dr. Moriah Hawkins, the cosmologist?"

"The same," Rachel returned.

"I heard her speak at our university twenty years ago when I was an undergraduate," Charlotte said. "She was absolutely brilliant!"

"She still is," I said, looking over my shoulder.

We found Moriah and von Kepler just finishing lunch. Moriah opened to us and I ushered Rachel and Charlotte through the door ahead of me. Charlotte was carrying her shopping bag containing the kettle and bell. Wasting no time, Rachel said, "We have a new wrinkle."

"Let's talk in the library," Moriah said.

When we were seated, Rachel said, "Professor Conrad is in the music department at St. Louis University."

"Marvelous institution," Moriah said, settling back in her chair and crossing her legs. "I spoke there once," she added.

"I was in the audience that day," Charlotte said. "I was a nineteen-year-old undergraduate. You were brilliant, Dr. Hawkins."

"Thank you dear."

"Professor Conrad has something to show you," Rachel said. Charlotte withdrew the kettle and bell from her Macy's bag. Moriah's chin rose slowly and she cast a look at von Kepler who passed a hand across his brow.

"I found these at my door early this morning in St. Louis," Charlotte began. "I went back inside and sat down. "When I rang the little bell, there was a knock at my door…"

Charlotte looked to Rachel, as though she needed a little help. Rachel only nodded.

"When I opened the door, a young woman in a lovely parka was standing there," Charlotte continued. "She told me that I must come to Hawkins Mill and speak with her friend Rachel Mountjoy. She said *we* are going to need my help. Who she meant by *we*, I don't know. Then she simply vanished before my eyes."

"There's to be a concert Christmas Eve in front of the store in town," Moriah said. "I think it's rather obvious, given the nature of your work at the university, that you've been drafted to conduct what we believe will be a children's choir."

"Where are the children from?" Charlotte asked.

"Excellent question," von Kepler said. "Unfortunately, we don't know as yet."

"How many members in the choir?" Charlotte asked.

"We've no idea," Rachel said. Suspecting that Professor Conrad's mind was reeling, Rachel looked to von Kepler for help.

"Some years ago, Moriah's theory that there is within the *vortex*—if you will—of a parallel universe living entities capable of materializing in what we in science call the classical world, shook academia to its foundations," von Kepler began. "As if that were not enough, our dear colleague——von Kepler shot a furtive look at Moriah who was quietly listening—added a prediction which, of course, must accompany any theory. She predicted that we are on the threshold of meeting such an entity. I needn't tell you what an uproar that created."

"The young woman I met is that entity?" Professor Conrad put in.

"Yes, we believe so," Moriah said. "What's more, we think that she is only an envoy, forward observer, perhaps I could say. Come Christmas Eve, she may very well waylay us with the unimaginable."

"It's hard for me to imagine that I would be needed to conduct a children's choir," Charlotte said. "Surely someone from your local school could do that."

"Evan and I have heard Hannah sing," Rachel said. "To say that she has a remarkable voice is far from adequate."

"You're losing me," Charlotte said.

"We're all a bit lost, dear," Moriah said. "But it's my guess that Hannah was sent to fetch you because of the level of conducting skill that will be needed."

Professor Conrad drew a deep breath and released it slowly. She searched the faces of us all then said, "Are you suggesting that I've been called upon to conduct a choir of ... of angels?"

"Something like that," Moriah said.

"Have you ever done it?" Rachel said, evoking much needed laughter and relief.

"I've had the privilege of conducting some great choirs and choral groups," Charlotte said, "but none of them had wings."

When more laughter subsided, Rachel said, "There's another name, entity, I should say, that's in the mix. I asked Hannah where she got the lovely coat. She said Missymammy made it for her. I asked if Missymammy sews. Hannah said sort of then twittered her fingers. I asked her who Missymammy is. She demurred and said just Missymammy. She takes care of us."

"Is anybody else in the community aware of what's going on here?" Charlotte said.

"Not that we know of," Rachel said. "I think that some have grown suspicious since Dr. von Kepler arrived. Then there was the reporter from *The New York Times*. We haven't seen him lately, but I doubt that he's gone far."

Rachel's last phrase turned out to be almost prophetic. We heard a knock on the front door. I opened to Charles Newton of the *New York Times*. He had a red kettle in his left hand and little bell in his right. I opened the door wider to allow him entrance. Inside, he gazed at everyone sitting in the room. He lifted the kettle and bell almost chest high and said, "Anybody else have a set of these—besides The Salvation Army, I mean?"

"Please come in and join us," Moriah said. I introduced the man. He took a seat and placed the kettle and bell in his lap, as though he were holding a child.

"May I ask where you got those?" Rachel said.

"I spent the night east of here, in West Plains," Newton began. "As I was leaving my hotel room to go downstairs for breakfast, I found these sitting just outside the door." He shifted the kettle and bell in his lap, causing the bell to ring slightly.

His attempt to continue his story was interrupted by the sudden appearance of Hannah at the entrance to the library. She was wearing her monk's robe. With both hands she gently pushed the robe's hood from her head then smoothed her blonde hair a little here and there. Her opulent, dark eyes swept us as she spoke: "I heard the little bell." She smiled then settled her gaze upon Charles Newton for a moment.

For all of his supposed interest in things paranormal, the man seemed to be paralyzed from the neck up. Finally he said, "It's nice to see you again, Hannah." The girl nodded then turned her attention to Professor Conrad who could only stare.

"Missymammy said that I should come and tell you that there is another person that we need."

"Who is Missymammy?" Newton said.

Hannah cut to him with a look that bordered on *none of your damn business.* "Just Missymammy," she said at last. Given the rather withering look in Hannah's eyes, Newton thought it best not to pursue the subject further at the moment. I thought that he had made a wise decision.

With the silencing of Charles Newton, Professor Conrad spoke: "I've learned that there is to be a concert in town on Christmas Eve. I'm only guessing, Hannah, that you and, well, Missymammy have called upon me to direct the choir. Is that correct?"

"Yes," Hannah said.

"May I ask how many singers there will be?" Charlotte

continued.

"Many," Hannah said.

"Children?" Charlotte continued, emboldened by the direct answers.

"Yes," Hannah returned.

This is getting better by the minute, I thought, opting to keep quiet for the moment.

The professor was on a role and she said, "Shouldn't we set aside some time for rehearsal?"

Hannah giggled and pushed a lock of blonde hair from her forehead. "We know all the music," Hannah said, folding her hands before her. "All you will have to do is stand before us and tell us what you want us to sing. Then wave your hands and stuff, you know like director's do, so that we do it the way you want. Some of the children sing too loud and try to take over. Hannah was silent for a moment then said, "Me and some of my friends saw you in the big hall in New York once."

"Carnegie?" Charlotte said.

"Yes," Hannah said.

Professor Conrad's eyes darted about the room then she said, "That—that was five years ago."

"Yes. We have been planning this for a long time," Hannah said. Rachel cut to me then to Dr. von Kepler who, like me, seemed to have decided to offer nothing unsolicited for the moment.

Professor Conrad appeared to have no more questions. Moriah spoke next: "I can't help but think that this concert is going to be about more than just entertaining our town Christmas Eve."

Hannah's eyes brightened. She seemed pleased that Moriah had cut to the chase. "Missymammy will speak when we are done singing," Hannah said.

I felt my pulse begin to race. I wanted to add something but didn't know what the hell it could be. Newton fidgeted in his chair and decided to risk another question: "Why have you called *me* here, sweetheart?"

"Please don't call me sweetheart," Hannah said with an edge in her voice.

"I'm sorry," Newton said.

"When Missymammy speaks," Hannah resumed, "you must write down what she says."

"And what am I to do with it?" Newton said.

"You will know after Missymammy speaks."

It was von Kepler's turn and he seized it: "May I ask you, dear—sorry, I didn't mean to say that … "

"You may call me dear, just not sweetheart—" Hannah said, breaking in. "Honey is okay, too, but not sweetheart. He—someone very bad called me that a long time ago."

I saw Rachel shift in her chair. She returned my glance and I saw something in her eyes that told me Hannah had sounded an alarm. I turned my attention to von Kepler who spoke: "What is my role in this?" he said somewhat haltingly.

"Missymammy says that the whole world knows how smart you and Moriah are. Without you, not many will believe. They will only laugh."

"What is my role, Hannah?" Rachel said.

"To be my friend."

"And mine?" I ventured.

"To love Rachel," Hannah returned.

No problem, I thought, while mine and Rachel's eyes met.

Rachel's lips parted as though she were going to speak again. She hesitated then said, "Hannah, the very bad person who called you sweetheart … what did he do to you?"

Such a cloud came over Hannah's face that I feared friendship had suddenly come to an end. The girl's breathing quickened. She began to tremble. Dishes rattled in the kitchen.

Half dozen books catapulted from the library shelves. I cut to Rachel. Her eyes were steady while she observed the girl's emotional violence. She began to calm, however, and I sensed that she would answer her friend. When the answer came, it shattered us all: "He raped me then choked me, to death. The last thing I heard him say was, "goodbye, sweetheart."

"My God," Professor Conrad mumbled. Rachel was so shaken that I sensed she would have given most anything to have her question back. She snuffed, pushed tears from her eyes and said in a voice that broke, "I'm sorry."

An awkward silence fell over the room while Hannah searched each of our faces, as if she were making a late hour assessment of our competence and whether or not we could be trusted to proceed in a way that we had been asked and nothing more. Just when we thought she was ready to make her exit, she withdrew a slip of paper from beneath her robe. "There's another person that we——I want. He will not come to you. You must go to him. This is directions so that you can find him," Hannah said, flourishing the slip of paper then laying it on a small table beside her. "You must all go together so that he will feel safe."

"Do you have a name for us?" Newton said.

"His name is Morgan," Hannah said.

"How old is he?" I asked in a follow up to Newton's question.

"I don't know," Hannah said. "Where I live, age isn't something we ever talk about."

Rachel had once told me that she asked Hannah how old she is and the girl said that she didn't know. It struck me as curious that Hannah knew her name but not how old she is. Time doesn't appear to be a factor in her dimension of existence.

With Hannah's announcement that there was another

subject, one that we must search for, I thought—mistakenly, once again—that it would possibly spell the end of this wild drafting of team members. "Missymammy would like for all of you to spend the night at the inn," Hannah said. "A man is coming to the inn at supper time. He will have a kettle and bell. He is a man of great influence, Missymammy says. But he will be very confused when you meet him. Please convince him that he's not crazy," Hannah said, giggling.

"How many more are coming?" I said, suspecting that I wouldn't get a definitive answer. I did, though, and it turned the heads of everybody in the room.

"Missymammy says this is all."

The girl left our midst in the same inexplicable way that she had arrived. We sat and stared at each other for long moments, as if she had turned us all into store mannequins. Rachel was the first to come to life. She rose from her chair and fetched the piece of paper that Hannah left for us. She stood in the middle of the room and perused the note.

"What does it say?" Moriah said.

"It's a partial map of St. Louis," Rachel said, still looking at the paper. "It's hand drawn. There's no address, just names of a couple of streets and what looks like an alleyway behind some shops. There's an arrow pointing to the alley. The letters WCA are inside of a square that has been penciled around it." She handed the paper to me. "I know where those streets intersect," she continued.

The words that had first haunted me at the beginning of all this raced through my mind like flood waters on Roubidoux Creek: *A voice is heard in Ramah, Rachel weeping for her children, weeping and great mourning, and she would not be comforted because they are no more.* Missymammy has something to say, Hannah told us. Given what we had heard of Hannah's trauma, I thought now that I had some idea of what it would be. And God help us all.

Moriah rose from her chair and said, "Well, I suppose I should go into the kitchen and see if any of my dishes are broken." The obvious practicality of those words in the aftermath of what we had witnessed set us all to laughing. Rachel began picking up the fallen books and returning them to their shelves.

When we had more or less recovered what remained of our wits, Moriah served us hot cider while we reached a consensus regarding our trip to St. Louis. We could load into Rachel's Jeep and go in the morning. Moriah wanted to fix Rachel, myself, and Charles Newton some lunch. And she had some flowers she wanted to take to the cemetery.

Ten

We reached the inn in the middle of the afternoon to await the arrival of the "man of great influence." We had lunch at Moriah's then went to the cemetery to lay flowers on Lilly and Rosie's graves. Her two husbands had plenty, she said. They had never been all that big on flowers anyway. Moriah was moving slower than usual on our way to the cemetery. I wondered if all the activity was taxing her a bit too much.

Upon our arrival at the inn, Professor Conrad got on her cell phone and called the university and arranged to be gone an extra day. Though she didn't divulge the nature of her need to be away from her office, she told us that she had no intention of being left out of the search for Morgan. Nor did she want to miss meeting the "man of great influence," she added, chuckling.

Rachel began to plan her menu for supper. Turning to me and Charles Newton, she said, "What do *men of great influence* like to eat?"

"I wouldn't have the foggiest idea," Newton said.

Rachel looked to me and I said, "I've never reached a level of influence that allowed me to be all that choosy."

Rachel laughed and said, "Well, I think I'll feed him pork loin and sweet potatoes. How does that sound to the rest of you?"

"I don't know where he's from," Charlotte said, "but I doubt that he'll turn his nose up on that."

"If he does, he can do without," Newton said.

We had no idea as to when our visitor would show up, nor did we know where he was coming from. I imagined that he had gotten no more detailed directions than those who had preceded him: Hawkins Mill, Missouri's Mark Twain National Forest. Our wondering and guesswork ceased when a call came from Gladys at the store. Rachel took the call and the conversation was brief as usual. We were all sitting about in the kitchen and Rachel turned to us and said, "That was Gladys at the store in town. She said that there are three people from New York asking to see me and Moriah. Gladys said they arrived in a limo."

"It must be our man of great influence," Charles Newton said. "I wonder if I know him," he added.

"Who could the other two be?" Charlotte said.

"We'll soon find out," Rachel said. It was decided that Rachel and I would go after our guests.

Arriving in town, Rachel wheeled the Jeep alongside a white limo bearing Missouri plates. We guessed that the car had been rented at an airport in Kansas City or St. Louis. We entered the store and found two men and a woman sitting at a table having coffee. Gladys was doing book work behind the counter. She smiled and nodded toward the visitors. The three deduced that Rachel and I had come to meet them. As we strode toward their table, they rose to greet us. A middle-aged man, whom I guessed was our man of great influence, was the first to extend a hand. "Rachel Mountjoy, I presume," he said.

"Yes," Rachel returned. "This is my friend Evan Van Clevin," she added.

The middle aged man introduced himself as Howard Smith. I put two and two together—Howard Smith and New York—and thought I knew who he was. Whatever Missymammy had to say, by God she was pulling all the stops in calling to Hawkins Mill the president of the country's largest T.V. Network. He introduced his companions as well. He looked to be in his late fifties, stoutly built, with short cropped graying hair. He was cleanly shaven. Thin lines at the corners of his eyes gave one the sense that he was a man capable of smiling, and often, though I saw no trace of humor in his face now. Pale brown eyes were alert and intelligent. He wore a navy blue business suit, finely tailored, I thought, given the excellent fit at the shoulders of the coat.

Standing beside him was a fellow that could pass for an NFL offensive lineman. He was black and I easily put him at three hundred pounds. He, too, was in coat and tie. I guessed him to be a bodyguard. Smith introduced him as Robert Janes.

The female, thirtyish, tall and fit was the man's secretary, I supposed. She was wearing a tweed skirt and sweater. She had lush, brunette hair. Blue eyes were intense. I thought I knew why. She had been introduced as Sally Horton.

When introductions had been made all around, Mr. Smith suggested that we talk in the limo. The bodyguard started the engine for running the heater. Comfortably seated, Rachel and I waited for the conversation to begin, though we thought we knew what it was going to be about, pretty much. Smith began by telling us who he was. I was correct. His professional identity out in the open, he proceeded to the purpose of his visit: "As I was leaving my home for the office early this morning, I found these sitting outside my door." He opened a small duffel sitting near his feet and extracted a red kettle and little bell. Rachel and I couldn't help but smile. Smith and his cohorts glanced at each other.

Smith continued: "I thought it was a gag, of course, or maybe a hint, being so near Christmas. I went back inside and set the things on a table. I gave the little bell a ring. When I opened the door to leave once more, a young woman was standing there. She was wearing a gorgeous parka with fur around the hood. She was quite beautiful. I was taken aback at first, suddenly seeing her standing just outside my door. I asked if I could help her in some way and she said 'I heard the little bell.' What is your name, dear? I said. 'Hannah,' she said."

Rachel and I glanced at each other again.

"I asked her if she knew anything about the kettle and bell I found at my door," Smith continued, "and she said yes, that she had left them. I was about to ask her why when she said that I must come to Hawkins Mill, in Missouri, in the Mark Twain National Forest and talk to Rachel Mountjoy and Moriah Hawkins. I was going to ask her why when she simply vanished before my eyes. Poof! She was gone. I'm hoping, Ms. Mountjoy, that you can tell me that I'm not losing my mind. Should that happily be the case, then perhaps you can tell me what is going on."

"We're not entirely sure ourselves," Rachel said. "The young woman, Hannah, has been gathering what appears to be a select group of individuals to Hawkins Mill: two journalists—one of them a Pulitzer winner; a Nobel Prize theoretical physicists from Heidelberg, Germany; and—just yesterday, a choral directory from St. Louis University; and now you, Mr. Smith."

I glanced at the secretary and she had begun to take notes furiously. The bodyguard had yet to say anything beyond what was spoken during the initial introductions.

"Do you have any clues as to what the purpose of this *gathering* is, Ms. Mountjoy?" Smith said.

Rachel deferred to me: "Are you familiar with the name Moriah Hawkins?" I said.

Smith rolled his eyes as though trying to call up the name. His secretary was well ahead of him and she said, "Didn't she teach at The University of Chicago, theoretical physics and cosmology?"

"Yes," I said, somewhat surprised at the young woman's memory. "She is best known for her theory—and prediction—

regarding parallel universe. To make a long story short, she predicted that there is within parallel universe—or, *universes,* living entities poised to make an appearance in our known world," I said, wishing that Moriah or Dr. von Kepler were here to help me, for I was attempting to swim in waters too damn deep for me. I kept stroking, dog paddling, however: "Moriah believes that her prediction has indeed been realized in the person of Hannah."

"And why has she come?" Smith said.

"Hannah has an accomplice, of sorts," Rachel said, mercifully giving me a breather from a subject much too difficult to parse for one so recently involved in the subject. "Someone whom she calls Missymammy appears to be pretty much calling the shots from behind the scenes, if I may put it that way."

Missymammy drew a smile from the bodyguard.

"We've been asked, of late, to have a concert on Christmas Eve, here in front of the store," Rachel continued. "Mr. Charles Newton from *The New York Times* has been asked to write down all that transpires."

"Who will be doing the singing?" Smith asked.

"A children's choir," Rachel said.

"And where are the children from?" Smith continued.

"From where Hannah has come, we're guessing," Rachel said.

"How large a choir is it?" the secretary asked, still taking notes and not looking up. I noted fine, brunette hairs trembling near her temples.

"Hannah says *many,*" I put in.

"Why have I been called?" Smith asked.

"Hannah says that Missymammy has something to say, presumably to the entire country, if not the world," Rachel said.

"I'm to broadcast this on my network?" Smith said, somewhat incredulously, glancing at his secretary and bodyguard.

"That's what we're thinking," Rachel said, smiling widely.

"If I hadn't witnessed the young woman's vanishing act before my very eyes," Smith said, "I would dismiss this out of hand as a hoax. I don't know what is going on here in this lovely little hamlet deep in your Mark Twain National Forest, but I aim to find out. Come Christmas Eve, my network will have state of the art production equipment on site. Is that what Hannah ... and Missymammy want?"

"We think so," Rachel said in a voice that broke with emotion. She looked at me with eyes that glistened with tears. Rachel cleared her throat then said, "There's one other person named Morgan whom we've not met. He isn't coming to us. We must go to him, somewhere in St. Louis. Hannah gave us a little map. We're leaving early in the morning."

"We would like to go along, if you don't mind," Smith said, glancing at his secretary and bodyguard.

"Yes, of course," Rachel said. "Your party may stay at my home tonight. There's going to be too many of us for my Jeep," she added. "Maybe we could take your limo."

"You got it," Smith said.

Rachel and I thought it not wise to put the limo through the woods along the wagon track. Our visitors each had a single bag and laptop satchel. After informing Gladys that the limo would remain in front of the store overnight, we loaded into the Jeep.

Arriving at our destination, we unloaded and ushered our guests to the front door and inside. Though they had remained politely quiet regarding the inn's rather shabby exterior, I saw astonishment on their faces as they cast about at the interior. "This used to be an inn," Rachel said. "I don't worry about the outside much anymore, but I've kept the inside nice."

"You have indeed," Howard Smith said.

Noting our entry, Moriah, Charlotte, Charles Newton, and Dr. von Kepler came from the kitchen and joined us in the foyer. Rachel began to make introductions. Newton had once appeared on one the network's programs after winning a Pulitzer. Smith recalled the segment and congratulated Newton. Sally Horton turned to Moriah and said, "It's an honor to meet you, Dr. Hawkins. Academia suffered a great loss upon your retirement. I can't imagine that The University of Chicago has recovered."

"You're much too kind," Moriah said.

Rachel and Charlotte excused themselves to begin preparing supper. The rest of us took seats in the great room. Moriah asked if I would bring in some wood and build a fire, designated fire builder that I am. The bodyguard offered to help. While gathering firewood, he said, "I used to live in Kansas City. I remember your column in the *Star*."

"Have you ever played football?" I said, glancing at the mountain of a man beside me.

"I played at Nebraska," he said, picking up an armload of firewood, seemingly unconcerned with the crumbs of bark on his suit coat. "I might have been drafted in the NFL but bad knees ended that."

"I'm sorry," I said.

"It happens," he said, turning as we made our way back to the house. "Mr. Smith is a generous man, and I don't have to get busted up on a line of scrimmage," he added, chuckling. "That makes my wife happy, but my boys wanted to see dad play."

"Rough way to make a living, football," I said.

"Yeah, but I loved the game."

I set to building a fire in the great room hearth. Moriah had found a wool shawl to wrap about her thin shoulders. She and von Kepler were fielding questions from Smith and his secretary. They wanted to know, of course—exactly, what is parallel universe. "I can't answer that question, and neither can anyone else at the moment," Moriah said. "It could have something to do with dark matter and dark energy that physicists are working very hard to understand. There could possibly be a relationship with the rather recently discovered Higgs boson particle that appears to have the capability of pulling dark matter into a mass."

"Why now, this extraordinary development?" Smith said.

"Everything has its time," Moriah said. "We know that evolution is still occurring. A species of fish has recently been observed in the process of evolving, and in a remarkable short period of time. We know that the universe continues to expand at breathtaking speed. I believe that our scientific knowledge, at least our willingness to believe in the *possibility* of parallel universe, may have reached a point where what has happened here with the appearance of Hannah will not necessarily be dismissed out of hand. Science must have evidence, however; we have that and then some with Hannah: cold, hard fact and truth, Mr. Smith. No one with a brain larger than a walnut will deny what we have seen."

"Is this simply about informing the scientific community?" Smith said.

"I think that Hannah—and Missymammy don't give a damn about the scientific community," Moriah said.

"What's the point, then?" Smith said.

"I spent my professional life dealing with theories," Moriah said. "I have one now. This home operated as an inn for three generations in Rachel's family. No more. For a terrible tragedy occurred here some years ago. A woman threw her child to her death from that balcony."

Moriah directed Smith's attention to the top of the winding staircase.

"The incident shattered Rachel," Moriah continued. "In an act of mental self-preservation, she got herself a kettle—painted it pink, a little bell, and began raising funds which she donates to organizations that help neglected and abused children. I myself went with Rachel that first day into town. That was the day Hannah appeared to us. 'I heard the little bell,' she said."

"That's what she said to me," Smith said.

"I think that the kettle and bell have nothing to do, really, with The Salvation Army," Moriah said, chuckling then glancing at the fire and drawing the shawl closer about her shoulders. "I believe that Rachel's profound pain and goodness struck a chord somewhere in another dimension. The kettle and bell are simply symbols of what she called into being. Perhaps all this was standing at a threshold, anyway. Rachel rang the little bell and said, in effect: *It is time, Hannah. Come to us.*"

"Beautifully put, Moriah," the secretary said softly.

"I think that one cannot find words for the beauty of what we will witness on Christmas Eve. I just hope I live that long."

"Are you not well?" Smith said.

"I'm older than the Big Bang, Mr. Smith. A hillbilly my age could kick off without notice."

"What are we going to hear on Christmas Eve?" Smith said, cutting to the chase.

"Music," Moriah said

"What else?" Smith said, unwilling to let Moriah off the hook.

"I believe that we—the country, all the world, perhaps— seeing that you have been called here—are going to face one of the greatest tragedies of our time in a way that we could never have imagined. America leads the industrial world in child abuse. And shame, everlasting shame on the man or woman who does not listen and turn from their reprehensible ways."

"God help us all," I mumbled in benediction.

Nobody sitting about in the great room needed much of an announcement regarding supper. The aroma coming from the kitchen had all of us salivating. The invitation came, however, and we took seats at the dining room table that had been set while the rest of us pondered deep mysteries unfolding in our midst.

Dr. von Kepler was obviously a man of prayer. For those of us who weren't particularly religious, his saying grace over the meal seemed most appropriate—welcomed as a kind of insurance—lest we inadvertently get on the wrong side of powers beyond us and knocking at our terrestrial door.

While pork loin, sweet potatoes, green beans, carrots, and dinner rolls were passed around the table, Howard Smith broached a question that none of us had thought to consider, or perhaps didn't care to, for long at least: "If what you believe will happen Christmas Eve does in fact occur, and our telecommunication technology captures it, have you considered what it will mean to Hawkins Mill should we broadcast the event?"

All of us sitting at table must have had a dumbfounded look on our faces; a classic case of having overlooked—or, denied the obvious.

While spreading margarine on a dinner roll, Smith rather casually told us what would happen: inundation. More people than fleas on the backs of every hound in the Ozark Mountains."

"Gladys will have to add on to her store," Moriah said in a casual tone that set us all to laughing.

"God help us all," Rachel said, kindly mimicking my soft but audible benediction just moments ago.

"Amen to that," von Kepler said, sampling his pork loin and glancing about the table.

Eleven

It was *6:00 a.m.* when we managed to get ourselves back into Rachel's Jeep and head into town to transfer into the limo for a considerably more comfortable ride to St. Louis and our search for Morgan. We had one less passenger; Charles Newton had to be back in New York but would return to Hawkins Mill for the concert. Robert Janes was driving and we directed him onto the state highway that would lead us to Interstate 44 and east to St. Louis.

Nearing our crossing at the Current River, we again saw the Guernsey cows making their way toward the milk barn. Rachel and I laughed at the timing. She informed our companions that she had gotten some of their milk and separated the cream. Fabulous!

Rachel had Hannah's sketchy map in hand. She said that the intersecting streets that we will be looking are on the city's southwest side. Though we feared that we might be looking for a proverbial needle in a haystack, not having to fight intercity traffic would be in our favor. "There's a long strip mall near this intersection," Rachel said. "The alley behind it may be what we're looking for."

"Why the alley?" Smith said.

"The WCA on the map, square penciled around it, may be a dumpster," Janes said.

"A dumpster?" Moriah said.

"Yes," Janes said, keeping his eyes on the road and passing a vehicle. "If I'm right, it may stand for Waste Corporation of America."

"Good Lord," Charlotte said. "We'll find Morgan in a dumpster?"

"It's possible," Janes said.

"I'd like to know how this fits into the scheme of things as we know it at this point," Smith said.

"Pieces keep falling into place," Rachel said. "Somebody knows what they're doing," she added.

"I'm glad somebody does," I said, evoking laughter from the rest of the party.

"How do we know we'll find anybody home?" Charlotte said.

"Take our chances, I guess," Smith said. "I've been on some adventures and excursions in my fifty some years, but this beats them all!"

Traffic became heavier as we entered St. Louis suburbs. Our driver moved to the right lane and stayed put so that we wouldn't be crowded out of our need to exit at the proper time when Rachel indicated. "Not much farther," she said.

Reaching our desired exit, Janes wheeled the limo off the Interstate. At the bottom of the ramp we waited on a red light. "About a mile from here is where we want to go," Rachel said. We proceeded when the light turned green and shortly Rachel directed our driver to turn into a lot hosting a strip mall and a dozen or more shops. Janes found a parking spot on the end of the strip nearest to us. We could see the alleyway.

"Well, what do you say we go look for our fellow Morgan?" Smith said, opening his door. When we had all exited the limo, drawing some looks from passersby, we walked to the alley and stopped. A considerable number of blue dumpsters with WCA painted on their sides were positioned along the alley.

"Here goes," Rachel said, stepping out down the alley while the rest of us followed. Reaching the first dumpster, we found its lid up. As though we feared something might leap from the container and grab us, we held back while Rachel looked inside. "No Morgan," she said, turning to us. We cast looks and faint smiles at each other.

"I can't believe we actually expect to find somebody in one of these," Charlotte said as we proceeded to the next dumpster some fifty feet away. We found the lid down on this one. Emboldened by Rachel, Charlotte knocked on the dumpster's lid and said, "Morgan, are you in there?" No answer. She lifted the lid a bit and looked inside. "Nothing but pizza cartons," she said, easing the lid closed.

We continued down the alley, dumpster after dumpster, and not finding what we were looking for. We had begun to think that either we read the map wrong, or Hannah had made a mistake. We were determined, though, to continue to the end of the alley.

Running out of dumpsters upon whose lid we could knock, we all stood about and wondered what had gone wrong. Rachel got out the map once more and we gathered near to look at it. We clucked our tongues, shrugged our shoulders and began making our way back to the limo. Midway in the alley, we heard movement inside a dumpster behind a shoe store.

Rachel rolled her eyes to us then knocked on the dumpster's lid and said, "Morgan, are you in there?"

"Who is it?" came the voice of a young boy.

"Oh, my God," Charlotte whispered putting a hand to her mouth.

Rachel cut to me and I could only shake my head in disbelief. "We're friends, Morgan," Rachel said.

"I don't have any friends."

"You do now," Rachel said. "We want to talk to you. Please open the door—lid."

We stood quietly for long moments while the dumpster's occupant considered Rachel's request. We heard what sounded like cardboard boxes being shuffled about. The dumpster's lid was in two half and one side eased up just a bit, cracked only an inch or so. We saw two eyes looking out at us. "Hi, Morgan," Rachel said, bending at the waist and peering into the crack.

"How do you know my name?" the boy said.

"A friend told us about you. She said we could find you here."

"Does she work in the shoe store?" the boy said.

"No," Rachel said.

"What do you want?"

"We have a better place for you to live," Rachel said.

In one moment in time, I thought that Rachel had committed to caring for this boy, spawned by unerring trust in Hannah and Missymammy's guidance.

"Does it stink?" Morgan said.

"No," Rachel said.

The rest of us couldn't help but smile at the course of this dialog. We wanted to see something other than two eyes, but dared not do anything more uninvited. The lid eased shut and we thought that perhaps that was the end of conversation. We heard movement inside once more, however, and the dumpster's lid began to open wide then was pushed upwards. I saw that as a measure of acceptance and stepped forward and took hold of the lid to keep it open. Morgan stood upright. He looked to be eight or nine years old. His hair was dark brown, dirty, and disheveled. Hazel eyes were large with bluish circles beneath them, created by the coldness of his home, I guessed. He was wearing a grey hoodie, quite filthy. The hood was down on his shoulders. Jeans, equally as filthy, were much too large for him and secured about his waist by a web belt. In spite of one eye that drifted outwardly just a bit, he was a handsome little guy with a fine forehead and strong chin. He had yet to smile, but his teeth, what we could see of them, were straight, albeit in need of brushing. His face and hands obviously hadn't seen a bar of soap for some time.

The boy searched each of our faces then fixed his gaze on Robert Janes and said, "Do you play for the Chiefs?"

"No," Janes said, breaking into a wide smile, "but I played for the Nebraska Cornhuskers when I was in college."

"I'm a Chiefs fan," Morgan said. "He reached down into the dumpster and picked up a sleeping bag, as well as a backpack with Chiefs colors and logo.

"I'm a Chiefs fan, too," Janes said. "Could I help you out of that dumpster?" he added.

"Okay," Morgan said, handing the sleeping bag to Rachel. He slung the backpack over one shoulder then extended his arms to Janes.

When the boy was standing on level ground, we all introduced ourselves to him. There was brief but awkward silence, as though none of us knew what to do next. I wished that Hannah were present to give us a little help. Rachel rose to the occasion, though, and she said, "Morgan, have you ever been to the Ozarks?"

"No."

"I have a big house there, so much room that I don't know what to do with. I wonder if you would like to stay with me for a while," Rachel said.

"Do you have a television so that I can watch the Chiefs?"

"Yes."

"Could I watch the Chiefs and have some pizza and pop?"

"Yes," Rachel said. I looked at the rest of the party and their eyes were misty. This boy had a small list. We knew, of course, that he was probably a runaway. Running from whom—or, what would have to be discovered. For now, though, getting him out of a dumpster was the first priority. I was certain of one thing: Hannah probably knew all there was to know about young Morgan.

First thing on our list, it seemed to me, was to get the boy something to eat. That occurred to Howard Smith and he said, "Well, what do you say we go get some lunch? It's about that time."

"Excellent idea," Charlotte said as we turned and headed for the limo. Morgan was wide eyed when it became apparent that it was our ride. Given the boy's filthy appearance, we deemed it best to find a drive thru for our lunch and eat it in the limo. And, while we were still in St. Louis, we would shop and get the boy some decent clothes to get into after a bath when we reached the inn.

After burgers, fries, and sodas—milkshake for dessert for Morgan—we found a department store. Charlotte, Rachel, and Moriah thought that they could manage the shopping without Morgan. They figured that store personnel wouldn't be too high on Morgan trying on clothes, dirty as he was. Looking him over to get a feel for his sizes, the three women exited the van and made their way into the store.

While the shoppers were gone, Smith, Janes, Sally Horton, von Kepler and I tried to keep a casual conversation going. We learned that the boy was 8 years old. We avoided questioning him further about his homelessness; we turned the conversation to football. Morgan knew that the Chiefs were in the playoffs after a long drought. His ability to rattle off player stats was remarkable. While shamelessly wolfing down the burger and fries, we heard not one word about his home in a dumpster or what he had been eating. I wondered what kind of home he had before that. Perhaps the dumpster was preferable. The kid was obviously tough as roofing nails.

I was a little nervous about snatching a minor into the limo and driving away with him. With the exception of my own mediocre credentials, I figured that the rest of the party would carry considerable weight should we be questioned by authorities. If we ended up in jail for kidnapping, Hannah better spring us.

Rachel, Moriah, and Charlotte returned with a cache of new clothes: jeans, underwear, socks, shirts, coat, sneakers, and a Chiefs hoodie that drew a beautiful smile from the boy.

It was an enjoyable ride back to Hawkins Mill. Morgan wanted to know who our friend was that told us about him. We said that we hoped he would meet her soon. After spending some time with this boy, it was my opinion that he could handle a sudden appearance of Hannah.

Moriah characteristically listened more than she talked. Morgan had taken a liking to her and he sat close, almost touching. The old woman, sensing his affection, took one of his hands, patted it then said, "How long have you been living in that dumpster, young man?" She had broken ice that the rest of us had been reluctant to try, lest we alarm the boy into thinking that he was going to be scolded and lectured to.

"For a couple of weeks," Morgan said. Moriah attempted to gently release his hand but he held on to her. She didn't resist. "I liked it because it only had dry stuff, cardboard boxes and paper. I jumped out, though, when I heard the trash truck coming. I heard of a homeless man in a dumpster who fell asleep or something and got dumped into the truck and smashed."

So forthcoming was the boy regarding his stay in the dumpster, Charlotte asked, "Do you have a mother and father or brothers and sisters in St. Louis?"

"I had a sister, but she died before I was born. My mom and dad are in jail for drugs. I lived in a foster home."

"Did you run away?" Sally Horton said, joining the conversation for the first time.

"I've been in lots of foster homes. I lived with five different families in six months. I decided that I would rather live on the street."

"Are the police looking for you?" Smith asked.

"Probably, but I'm very tricky. I heard one of you knock on the dumpster and ask if I was in there. When I heard footsteps coming down the alley, I crawled under the boxes. I thought it might be the police." With that, Morgan picked up his new Chiefs hoodie and ran his hand across the arrowhead logo. He pulled the hoodie to his chest, as though it were a security blanket. He leaned against Moriah and gazed out of the window and seemed to not care to talk anymore for now. Ignoring the boy's dirty hair, Moriah stroked his head. He closed his eyes and was soon sound asleep.

Having gotten up so early and enduring the stress of searching dumpsters, most of us in the limo could have easily taken a nap. I did in fact nod off. I was brought back when Rachel nudged me and said, "We have company." I opened my eyes to see Hannah sitting across from me.

"I see that you found him," she said. She glanced to the front of the limo at our driver who was mumbling and alternating his attention between the road and rearview mirror.

"Yes, we found him where you said he would be," Rachel said. "He's terribly dirty, as you can see. We bought him some new clothes and shoes. He'll get a bath when we get to the inn."

"Good," Hannah said. She looked toward the front of the limo and said, "Thank you, Mr. Janes, for helping to find Morgan. I'm Hannah," she added.

"No problem," Janes said, taking a deep breath and releasing it with a rush as he gave his full attention to the road ahead.

"It's nice to see you again, Mr. Smith," Hannah said. "Missymammy wanted me to thank you for agreeing to bring your television stuff to Hawkins Mill for our Christmas Eve concert."

"We'll be there, dear, and with the best technology available,"

Smith said. "We'll wake up some satellites, I guarantee."

Hannah smiled then turned her attention to Morgan who was sleeping soundly. "You all are probably wondering why I wanted you to find Morgan," she said.

"We are indeed," von Kepler said.

"Morgan is my brother," Hannah said.

This story is taking on more twists and turns than the road I got lost on, I thought. All of us in the limo were struck dumb as marionettes thrown into a trunk. Hannah sensed as much and she began to enlighten us: "Morgan and I have the same mother, different fathers. Morgan was born after I died. He doesn't know how I died. It would have hurt him very much, I think."

"It hurts *us* very much too," Charlotte said.

"I've kept track of Morgan and I wanted to find a way to get him to be with me, but there was nobody I trusted, until I met Rachel. When I found out that Morgan ran away from his foster home, I had to do something to get him out of that dumpster. Missymammy and I thought this would be the perfect time to bring him here."

"He may stay with me as long as he wants," Rachel said.

"Oh, thank you, Rachel," Hannah said. "Now I can come and see him whenever I like."

"What will he think when he sees how you are, you know, the way you—" Rachel said then trailing off.

"He'll say awesome!" Hannah said with a broad smile. "I know my brother. He'll think it's the coolest thing ever!"

"It is the coolest thing ever," I said.

"Seriously cool," Janes said from the driver's seat, evoking laughter from the rest of us.

Morgan began to stir from his nap. "I better go for now," Hannah said. With that, the seat where she sat became empty. "No matter how many times I see her disappear like that,"

Rachel said, "it always takes my breath."

"If anything like that happens come Christmas Eve, there's going to be a lot more breathless people," von Kepler said. "It will blow paranormal skeptics out of the water. And it will get you a ticket to Stockholm, my dear," he added, looking at Moriah who was attempting to smooth Morgan's hair as he sat up from his nap.

"I'm too old for a Nobel Prize," Moriah said. "Anyway, I don't have enough years left to spend that kind of money."

"It's a lot of dough," von Kepler said, he himself having been given a Nobel for physics. "I bought a new car and better furniture for my study, that's about it."

Fully awake, Morgan sat up straight and said, "Are we there yet?"

"Almost," Rachel said. "We've got to go into town and get my Jeep."

Upon reaching Hawkins Mill, Charlotte Conrad said, "I need to get back to the university. I've got a couple of ensemble concerts to conduct on campus. Fortunately I've nothing scheduled Christmas Eve, so I'll be back as early in the day as I can for our big bash here." She shook hands all around, gave Morgan a hug then got into her car and drove away.

As we stood in the street and watched her drive out of sight, Howard Smith said, "Hannah and Missymammy have certainly done their homework. That woman is considered to be one of the finest choral conductors in the country."

Smith and his small entourage bid us farewell. He said that his secretary would arrange for the production equipment for the concert and it would be flown into Kansas City. It would be arriving in Hawkins Mill in a couple of days. Production staff would be housed in RVs. He hoped that Gladys' store had plenty of coffee on hand, he added, chuckling. Robert Janes, opening a door in the limo for Smith and his secretary, turned to Morgan and said, "Go Chiefs!"

"Go Chiefs!" Morgan returned with a broad smile. He raised his right hand and gave Janes a Chiefs chop. Janes gave one back as he closed the limo door then took his place behind the wheel.

After the limo had driven away, Rachel said, "I think we better alert Gladys to the production crew that's coming. She may want to stock up."

Inside the store, we introduced Morgan. Gladys' face blanched at the boy's appearance, but otherwise concealed her thoughts. "Mr. Smith, the man from New York, is head of a large T.V. network and he's sending production equipment to cover our Christmas Eve concert," Rachel said.

"Oh my goodness," Gladys said.

"The equipment and crew will be arriving in a couple of days," Rachel continued. "Mr. Smith hopes that you have plenty of coffee. He said that the crew will be staying in RVs."

"I've got another urn I can put out," Gladys said, glancing toward the single copper coffee urn. "I better get on the phone and order in some extra groceries from my supplier."

"Good idea," Rachel said.

"I'll spread the word around town," Gladys said.

Leaving the store, we loaded into the Jeep and headed for Moriah's place to drop her and Dr. von Kepler off.

Leaving Moriah's home, we took the trail through the woods to the inn. "Where are we?" Morgan asked while he gazed out of the Jeep's windows.

"In the Ozarks and the Mark Twain National Forest," Rachel said.

"Are we lost or anything?"

"No, and we'll be home soon."

"Home," Morgan said just above a whisper while taking in the densely forested landscape.

When we reached the inn, we gathered up Morgan's new clothes and went inside. "Wow, this is where you live?" the boy said, standing in the foyer and looking about him.

"This is it," Rachel said.

Rachel suggested that I help our guest with a bath. That I did and when we returned from an upstairs bathroom, Morgan wearing new clothes, Rachel could hardly believe that he was the same boy.

Christmas was less than a week away. Time to put up her Christmas tree, Rachel said. After an early supper, we would do just that. What occupied our thoughts at the moment, however, was a need in the not too distant future to get in touch with child welfare authorities and notify them that Morgan was in safe keeping. In the meantime, we would have to give some thought as to how it was that we happened to stumble onto him in a St. Louis dumpster. Telling them that a *ghost* led us to him wouldn't do. Should we be successful in explaining our innocents in rescuing Morgan, I thought that Rachel would have little or no trouble qualifying as a foster home for the boy, if in fact that was on her mind. I believed that it was. That he was Hannah's brother still had my mind reeling. When and how she would disclose the sibling phenomenon would be most interesting, not to mention Morgan's reaction to it.

Twelve

Rachel, Morgan and I rose early Christmas Eve. We had breakfast then drove into town to see how final preparations were coming along.

Howard Smith's T.V. network production crew had arrived two days earlier. Satellite dishes were pointing to the sky. There was a constant hum of generators from RVs and the Command Center. Townsfolk erected a Christmas tree across the street from Gladys' store. Local men had gone into the forest and cut a fifteen-foot yellow pine. The Mark Twain being a national forest, they might have needed to get permission. But they thought it would be okay, probably, given the nature of the occasion. Citizens turned out en mass to help decorate the lovely conifer. Children strung popcorn and cranberries. Families brought some of their most prized ornaments to hang on the tree. Tiny, multicolored twinkling lights hung from every bough.

Making our way into the store, we found it buzzing with customers. Gladys had brought in more tables and hired some local college girls to help. She had set a table with an assortment of donuts, rolls, and cakes, compliments of her store. Rachel and I got ourselves coffee, hot chocolate for Morgan and donut for each of us then managed to find a table. We hadn't been sitting long when we saw Charlotte Conrad walk in. We gained her attention. She found herself coffee and a donut then joined us. "I thought it would be a good idea to get here early," she said, dunking her donut into her coffee and looked about at the crowd. "You would think they are expecting the President!" she added.

"This town will never be the same," Rachel said.

"Good and bad, I guess. The local economy will get a rather permanent shot in the arm, though," I said.

We had learned through phone conversations with Dr. von Kepler that a team of scientists from several major universities, NYU among them, were on site to view firsthand what was purportedly to take place. We suspected that Charles Newton had tipped off NYU and the word had spread like a virus throughout academia. They had brought with them linguists who would monitor any unknown dialects or language. I asked Professor Conrad what she had in mind for music. Since this was to be broadcast from America's heartland, if in fact Howard Smith did make a decision to do just that, she thought it best to stick to traditional holiday songs familiar to the English speaking world.

We were a little anxious about when the choir members would arrive. Nor had we so much as a clue regarding how many there would be, if risers would be needed and where to station them. Hannah had only said that they would arrive at dark. Wait and see is all we could do. Turning to Charlotte, I said, "Are you getting nervous?"

"Nervous? Oh, that's putting it mildly," she said. "I'm scared absolutely witless! I thought that stepping on stage in front of a choir at Carnegie Hall was scary. That was back porch jam session compared to this."

I glanced at Morgan who was taking this all in rather quietly while he enjoyed his hot chocolate and donut. We had not yet told him about Hannah. We opted to let him witness for himself the evening's extraordinary event and get his reaction.

We were going to pick up Moriah and von Kepler at four o'clock so as not to expose the two of them—especially Moriah—to too much drilling from the scientists and media ahead of the actual concert; she had been looking awfully tired.

We figured that daylight savings time would put us in darkness somewhere between five and five-thirty in late December. Usually one might be hoping for at least a moderately white Christmas, but given the out of doors nature of this event we were glad to have been spared snowfall.

We returned to the inn, had an early lunch, and touched up the Christmas tree in killing a little time before returning to town.

At four o'clock we went after Moriah and von Kepler.

Upon reaching Moriah's home, we found the two of them ready and waiting. Each had a folding chair and a blanket. Noting that dusk was falling fast, Rachel wheeled the Jeep around and headed for town. "What's it like in there?" Moriah said.

"We'll soon find out," I said.

When we arrived in town we had to park a block away from the store. Hawkins Mill was fast becoming wall to wall and curb to curb people.

Reaching the network Command Center on foot, we thought that would be a good place to observe the concert. Howard Smith noted our arrival and strode over to greet us. Sally Horton, his secretary, and Robert Janes were in tow. Charles Newton from *The New York Times* had made it back into town and he was with Smith. A table was set up in front of the command trailer. A man and woman, network anchors who were household names, came from the trailer and took a seat. Staffers busied themselves around them, wiring them for sound, adding a touch more makeup, and providing a Thermos of coffee. I noted that an EMS unit had moved into position that gave them a good vantage point. Howard Smith had directed his secretary to request it. St. Luke's Hospital was emblazoned across the ambulance sides.

Smith had pulled all the stops. There were more cameras

than at an NFL game. In addition to a row of them stationed near where we stood and looking east down Main Street, cameras flanked both sides of the crowd whose numbers were growing and fast. Nothing would escape their lens. Wherever the choir emerged, the cameras would pick them up.

We judged that darkness was no more than twenty or thirty minutes off. Hannah had said that the choir would show up at dark. Street lights were on. Smith broached the question for a possible need of additional lighting for the choir. Moriah told him that they wouldn't be needed. She cut to von Kepler and he smiled and nodded.

The great crowd out in front of us was milling about and chatter was a dull roar. "I think we should risk making an announcement and tell people that the choir will arrive shortly," Smith said. "Perhaps that will settle them down. I think that it's appropriate, Ms. Mountjoy, for you to speak to them." Rachel agreed.

Smith asked a staffer to provide Rachel with a microphone. Taking the mic in hand, she began to speak: "Good evening ladies and gentlemen. I'm Rachel Mountjoy and I'd like to welcome you all to Hawkins Mill for tonight's concert. We expect the choir to arrive at any moment. We hope that you will enjoy the music."

People who had brought along folding chairs were seated on sidewalks. Those who chose to stand were mostly in the middle of the street. None of us had any idea how many choir members we could expect nor did we know where they would emerge from. After Rachel's announcement, people were looking all about them, wondering where the music would be staged. We ourselves had no answer. We could only wait.

When hearing Rachel's announcement, Charlotte Conrad sought us out and joined us. It was my guess that the temperature was somewhere in the mid 20s. There had been no wind, fortunately, so wind chill was not a factor. A breeze had begun to rise, however, but curiously enough it was bringing warm air. I looked to the sky then at Newton who was standing beside me. "The last thing we need is a storm," he said, looking to the sky and movement in the trees now barren of foliage. The wind didn't stiffen, but the temperature continued to rise. I undid the top button of my coat. Newton followed with the same. I looked to where Moriah and von Kepler were sitting and they had removed the blankets that had been about their shoulders and on their laps.

The breeze was very slight now. The temperature had settled to what I guessed was close to a comfortable 70 degrees with virtually no humidity ... on the 24th of December, deep in the Missouri Ozarks. I would have to consult a meteorologist as to whether or not this was some kind of record. Perhaps it wasn't. But the sudden rise in temperature was striking. I looked out across the crowd and saw people unbuttoning their coats. I glanced at Moriah and she smiled then said, "Maybe it's a gift from Missymammy."

If the rise in temperature was remarkable, what began to occur next would defy the greatest of imaginations. Snowflakes began to appear, and in a star studded sky. The flakes were huge, big as half dollars, I thought. But there was translucence about them as they shimmered their way to earth. I reached for one as it passed before me and it eluded my grasp. Children in the crowd were doing the same and oohs and aahs were coming from them. Howard Smith's jaw had come ajar. He looked to Moriah and she said, "*Virtual* snowflakes; a little something extra from Missymammy for the occasion." I heard gasps come from the crowd and turned to see a shooting star—the likes of which I have never witnessed—crossing the sky in almost slow motion, as if it meant for all the earth to note its presence.

When the virtual snowflakes had begun to appear, Howard

Smith fairly shouted, "Get on the air!" Camera personal hit the decks running. They closed in on the anchors as well as the great crowd out in front of us and the magnificent shooting star. I thought for a wild moment that maybe the world was getting ready to end and what we were seeing was a final goodbye. Given Smith's command to get on the air, it was obvious that he had made a decision to risk going live.

The anchors responded to Smith's cue: "Good evening," the male anchor began first. "We're coming to you this Christmas Eve from an undisclosed location deep in Missouri's Mark Twain National Forest. There's to be a concert staged here shortly. We are experiencing phenomena at this moment. It is, of course, the 24th of December and we are in America's heartland. But the temperature has risen to a very pleasant 70 degrees. What's more, snowflakes have begun to fall. But they are not your usual snowflakes. They are large, quite beautiful, as we hope you can see upon your television screens. But they are *virtual* snowflakes."

The female reached to grasp one of the flakes and it eluded her touch.

"We have just witnessed a shooting star cross the heavens," the female anchor began. "I have never seen one so huge and moving so slowly …"

The anchor's voice trailed off at the sound of gasps once more rolling across the crowd. On the eastern end of Main Street choir members had begun to arrive. They weren't getting off of buses. They were simply *materializing* before our eyes in the same way that we had seen Hannah do. Such a roar was coming from the crowd that I feared a stampede. But there was no indication that anybody was going anywhere. They stood and stared and turned their heads in wonder to each other. Some dropped to their knees and lifted hands toward the heavens.

"The choir members have begun to arrive," the female anchor said in a voice that broke with emotion. "What you're seeing is not a hoax," she assured television viewers.

The singers were dressed in white robes. I saw no wings on their backs; they may have been left behind for this occasion, I thought with tongue in cheek. My heart was pounding so fast that I felt a little light headed. I glanced at the EMS unit and hoped they wouldn't be attending me.

The singers seemed to be pouring out of the atmosphere. I cut to the multiple cameras on either side of me and those flanking the crowd. They were being manned; state of the art lenses moved in and out slowly as they sought ever better focus. "Jesus, Joseph, and Mary!" cried someone whose face was glued behind his camera; evidence that what was occurring was indeed being captured.

"Have we got sound?!" Howard Smith barked.

"You won't need it," Moriah informed rather casually.

Staffers who broke for the choir with wireless mics and stands halted upon hearing Moriah. Smith cut to her and she said, "We'll have all the sound we need."

"Somebody start counting!" Smith barked out again.

"I'm at 80 and counting!" cried a staffer.

"We've received no word regarding number of choir members," the male anchor said, "but they continue to arrive, as you can see. One of our staff is counting and is at 80. But they are still coming."

"I've got 150!" shouted the counter again.

"That's what I've got!" shouted a backup.

Given the youthful faces of the singers, I found it difficult to distinguish boys from girls. But I guessed that their ages ranged from about 3 years old to 15 or 16. They certainly were not novices, for they were taking their places in banks and tiers that indicated that they knew where their voice parts were to be located. They had no risers for such elevated positioning. They were apparently levitating to assume the proper balance.

"What's the count?!" Smith cried.

"300!" the counter called out above the roar of the crowd that was near deafening.

"Same here!" cried the backup.

When the singers finally quit emerging, the counter said, "We've got 360!" A full circle, I thought; a figure of completeness. Scanning the choir's faces, it seemed to me that they were of every race.

When all of the singers were in place, they remained motionless; waiting for their director, I supposed. It had become obvious to the crowd that the choir members above the first row were levitating to reach and maintain their proper arrangement. Many in the crowd had their hands over their mouths in shock at what they were seeing. I looked to Professor Conrad. Tears were standing in her eyes. Her head was trembling ever so slightly. "Your choir awaits you, professor," Rachel said.

Charlotte dashed at tears and said, "I ... I can't do this."

"They're waiting," Rachel said gently.

"I can't conduct a choir of angels!"

"We don't know that they are angels," Rachel said consolingly.

"Well, look at them! There are no risers. They're *floating* in their places for God's sake!"

"Hannah summoned you because you are one of the finest choral directors in America, professor. Don't disappoint her," Rachel said.

Charlotte snuffed and swiped at tears on her cheeks. She drew a deep breath and released it, blowing out her cheeks then turned to von Kepler, "Please pray for me," she said while she took off her coat, revealing a white Cashmere turtleneck sweater and grey, wool slacks.

"I will," von Kepler said.

Charlotte cast us all a final look then began to make her way toward her singers. She began walking rather slowly, haltingly at first. But her stride became more and more resolute as she made her way down the middle of the street while the crowd opened a way for her, like waters parting for Moses. Realizing that she must be the director, they broke into applause and cheers. "God bless you, dear," some said who were closest as she passed. She touched hands that were outstretched to her.

"Professor Charlotte Conrad from St. Louis University is now making her way through the crowd," the male network anchor said. "She will conduct the choir."

I saw Hannah standing in the middle of the sopranos. Charlotte saw her too and nodded and smiled, albeit weakly. The girl smiled and twitted her fingers.

Charlotte stood quietly and gazed at the enormous choir before her. I suspected that she was reminding herself that she had no orchestral accompaniment; pure a cappella. I wondered what her first selection would be. The crowd had grown still when she squared her shoulders and announced: *Carol of the Bells.* Her choir smiled in approval. I know this to be a rather difficult carol in terms of its blistering pace. It barrels like a rollercoaster to the end, often leaving singers short of breath. It certainly taxes my modest violin skills.

Charlotte raised her right hand and poised it to alert the choir. When her hand swept upwards and toward her singers, what came forth must have shaken her musical instincts to their very foundations, it did mine. The children picked up the carol's demanding cadence and timing with stunning precision. Their voices seemed to ring out across the heavens to the joy of the crowd:

Hark! how the bells
Sweet silver bells
All seem to say
Throw cares away
Christmas is here
Bringing good cheer
To young and old
Meek and the bold
Carol of the bells

Charlotte's trepidation was short lived. Her body language told me that she had summoned the energy and confidence this event demanded. When she gestured with her hands and facial expressions seeking more from her sopranos, altos, or tenors—even base, given the youth of the boys, they responded with immediacy. The mixing of the voices of the very young produced a sweet harmony that I had never heard. A girl, looking to be no more than three years old with red hair and green eyes was positioned on the first row. She was singing her heart out. Adding an orchestra would have been a travesty, I thought. The whole earth seemed to dance with the children's singing. When Charlotte signaled for her youngest members to take up the ding, dong, they snatched it and ran, even reversing the second line to Dong, ding, dong, ding to the crowd's delight:

Ding, dong, ding, dong
Dong, ding, dong, ding
That is the song
With joyful ring all caroling

One seems to hear words of good cheer
From everywhere, filling the air

O, how the pound, raising the sound
Over hill and dale telling the tale

Gaily they ring, while people sing
Songs of good cheer, Christmas is here
Merry, merry, merry Christmas
Merry, merry, merry, merry Christmas

On, on they send, on without end
Their joyful tone to every home

Charlotte brought the rollicking carol to a decisive close at the end of the 5th stanza. The crowd broke into thunderous applause. She turned toward the audience and swept her left hand toward her singers.

When the applause had quieted, the director's next carol slowed the tempo considerably with a lovely, easy flowing French carol: "*Quelle est cette Odeur,*" she announced to her choir. In English, I suspected. I was correct. She raised both of her hands, prompting her singers and they responded:

Whence is the goodly fragrance flowing,
Stealing our senses all away,
Shepherds, in flow'ry fields of May,
Never the like did come a-blowing,
Whence is that goodly fragrance flowing,
Stealing our senses all away.

While the crowd responded with more applause, Charlotte immediately embarked in the midst of the applause and sent her choir into *The First Noel* which they took it up without a hitch:

The first Noel, the Angels did say
Was to certain poor shepherds in fields as they lay
In fields where they lay keeping their sheep
On a cold winter's night that was so deep.
Noel, Noel, Noel, Noel...

On the last Noel, Hannah hit a high C that blew out a street light. Her fellow choir members put hands over their ears and frowned at Hannah. Charlotte motioned with her left hand for her principal soprano to hold it down. I looked at Rachel and she said, "She's such a show off. I knew she would do that!"

The audience cut to the shattered light while their applause rang out as Charlotte ushered her brilliant choir into a wonderful medley of the most beloved carols of all time: *Hark the herald Angels sing; O, Holy Night; Carol of the animals; How far is it to Bethlehem?; God rest ye merry gentlemen; Silent night, Holy night; We Three Kings of Orient Are; Angels from the Realms of Glory; Joy to the World.*

Never in my lifetime had I known such musical feasting. And it wasn't over. Charlotte took her choir into a medley of more contemporary songs: *I'm Dreaming of a White Christmas; Silver Bells;* and *Winter Wonder Land.*

Throughout the program, the anchors made subdued comments, one of which was that the choir members had no songbooks.

I was as caught up in the music as anyone, but lurking in the back of my mind was when Missymammy would appear and what she would have to say. We had been given as generous a concert as one could imagine. I looked at my watch. The children had been singing nonstop for nearly an hour. I sensed that the end was drawing near. It was. Charlotte brought the music to a close and turned to face the great crowd whose applause rolled like thunder. Those sitting in folding chairs came to their feet in ovation that I thought would never end.

When the ovation subsided and the crowd became quiet, we heard something more from the choir: "Missymammy comes," they said in a voice that seemed as one. At ground level, next to Charlotte Conrad, a figure began to materialize.

"Missymammy comes," the choir said again, softer this time in reverent tones.

When her arrival was completed, we saw a tall figure. She was wearing a hooded robe, the color of which was deep purple with white piping. The hood was up and we could not see her face. A question that was on Howard Smith's mind when he said to a cameraman nearby: "Can you see a face?"

"No. There is a glow, possibly coming from the eyes."

Missymammy was not alone, however. Coming in her wake were children, arriving two abreast. Each pair carried between them a small coffin, suitable for that of a very young child or baby. As they ranged themselves on either side of Missymammy, she spoke something to Charlotte who bowed slightly then stepped to one end of the choir. Everyone who had been sitting in folding chairs along the sidewalk continued to stand.

The choir members spoke again: "Missymammy loves. Missymammy loves."

She turned to her choir, raised her hands and put them together, as if blessing the singers then turned to face the audience and cameras. When she spoke, what we heard was in English, but there was inflection in her voice that I myself had never heard; I couldn't place it north, south, east, or west. There was remarkable gentleness, a plaintive cry, though her voice was level, and it seemed to surround us, coming from every direction. I cut to the covey of linguists. Their headphones were in place and they were shooting looks at each other, shaking their heads in obvious dismay.

"These children, whom I have sent to sing for you, were once neglected, abused and killed by their abusers," Missymammy began. "Shame, such unspeakable shame," she cried in a voice that seemed to ring down the corridors of eternity.

I heard Rachel snuff. I looked at her and tears were standing in her eyes. I could hear isolated weeping breaking out in the crowd. Dr. von Kepler and Moriah had gotten out of their chairs and were standing while they clung to each other's arm. This concert wasn't free, I thought. Missymammy is exacting a terrible price.

"You have heard how beautifully they sing," Missymammy continued. "Look upon their faces, all who inhabit the earth, and see what has been lost, what can never be recovered. As babies, some were shaken until little brains could take no more. Others were drowned, scalded, starved, put into cages and locked in dark places where their cries for help could not be heard."

"Dear God! No!" screamed a female voice in the crowd. The woman seemed to have collapsed. I could see EMS personnel rushing through the crowd.

I for one was hoping this crushing litany would soon end. I could hear emotional stress in Missymammy's voice as it rose and fell with every indictment. Weeping across the crowd had intensified. In what struck me as surreal, the choir members were swaying back and forth gently and humming just beneath Missymammy's voice. It felt as if the singers were offering a little merciful relief from the cosmic flogging being delivered by their beloved leader. At intervals they would repeat, "Missymammy loves." I couldn't identify the music they were humming in almost chanting cadence. I looked at the bank of linguists and they were shaking their heads at each other.

Missymammy wasn't done.

"Precious and tender limbs were broken; some were savaged in brutal sexual assault; and others——rather than face another day at the hands of their abusers——took their own lives. Look upon them now, peoples of the world. They are well and safe in my presence. But they wanted to live in your world, for it was their world too. They wanted happy childhoods. They wanted to grow and love and marry and have families of their own. But they were denied. Shame! Let everlasting shame rest upon the abuser!" Missymammy cried.

She became silent and God knows we all prayed that she was done. She was, almost.

"No more!" she hissed. "Abuse and kill no more!" With that she turned toward the choir and raised her hands in a kind of benediction, I thought. The choir ceased its swaying back and forth and humming. She turned to her young pallbearers and they began to disappear, one by one. The choir remained. Missymammy turned to face us once more and spoke: "Moriah, please come and bring your friends with you."

We looked at each other as if hoping one or the other would be the first to step forward. "Let's go," Moriah said at last. Rachel and I walked on either side of her with our arms entwined in hers; von Kepler and Morgan trailed along behind.

As we made our way down the middle of the street, the crowd, now grown deathly still, parted for us. "God bless you," many said softly as we passed.

When we reached where Missymammy stood, we still couldn't see her face, for the hood to her robe was pulled forward. There was a soft glow, however; her eyes, I guessed. I glanced at Rachel and she was fixed on a small choir member, a girl, standing on the bottom row. She had red hair and beautiful green eyes. "It's Rosie," Rachel said just above a whisper. The girl smiled and twittered her fingers at Rachel who returned the gesture.

I looked into an upper tier of the choir where Hannah had been stationed. She was gone. Out of the corner of my eye I saw movement off to the left of the bottom row of the choir near where Rosie stood. It was Hannah and she was coming toward us. She had an infant in her arms and it was wrapped in a white blanket. Hannah came to Moriah and stopped. She gently removed the covering from the infant's face and said, "Lilly, Moriah."

Rachel and I held Moriah's arms and we felt her knees begin to buckle. We firmed our hold and held her upright. She began to tremble. Missymammy stepped closer to Hannah. She extended her right hand from the full sleeves of her robe. The hand was as beautiful as fine porcelain. She touched the baby's head and a change in the infant's appearance began to occur. The child was being transformed from a three dimension image to what could be touched by human hands. Lilly's eyes were open. She reached a tiny hand and took hold of Moriah's finger and said, "Momma."

"You may hold her," Hannah said. Moriah took Lilly into her arms. The pitiful sounds coming from Moriah had my eyes so full of tears that I could hardly see. I swept them away and held on to the old woman as best I could. But she was falling and Rachel and I gently laid her on the street while the infant remained in her arms. I took off my coat and made a pillow for her. I could see a rapid rise and fall of her breathing while she held the baby and stroked its head. Her breathing became increasingly labored. I turned to Morgan and told him to go get someone from the ambulance. He broke into a sprint and soon returned with two EMS technicians. They dropped to their knees and tended to the old woman who was drawing her last few breaths.

Tears were pouring from Rachel's eyes. "Please don't go,

Moriah," she cried. I put an arm around her as we gazed into Moriah's face. Hannah gently took the infant from its mother's arms.

Moriah grew still. One of the EMS personnel kneeling beside her looked up and said, "She's gone."

Moriah was taken away. Her passing would be properly recorded then her body transferred to a nearby funeral home.

Rachel, Morgan, von Kepler and I returned to where Howard Smith was standing. We had no need to tell him of what had occurred; his camera crew had captured it all.

"We've just heard that the music and Missymammy's words were instantaneously translated into every known tongue," Smith said. "Missymammy's doing, I'm guessing."

The days that followed the concert were most interesting. We learned from Howard Smith that the exact location of the concert had still not been disclosed in order to avoid— hopefully—absolute tidal wave of humanity pouring into tiny Hawkins Mill. Somewhere deep in Missouri's Mark Twain National Forest, is all that continued to be said. They began to find us, though, in moderate numbers at first. We suspected that those numbers would grow and for a very long time.

Gladys' store had generated quite a lot of money during the run up to the concert. She secured local carpenters and began preparations for a sidewalk café just outside her store. It would be ready in the spring. She was going to add a second floor that would house a bistro with a balcony that looked out onto the site where the choir and Missymammy once were. A great bolder of limestone was trucked into town and a bronze plaque was mounted on it, marking the spot where Missymammy and the choir had appeared. The City Council was in unanimous agreement, however, that no permits would be given to build hotels or any other new structures. Gladys' store and other businesses would be allowed to expand and remodel a bit. The community wanted Hawkins Mill to remain pretty much as is.

Word came from Stockholm, Sweden that Dr. Moriah Hawkins had been nominated for a Nobel Prize in physics, posthumously. No one entertained for a moment that Moriah would be denied the prize. Rachel and I would be going to the ceremony on Moriah's behalf.

Moriah willed her home and forty acres to the town of Hawkins Mill. She stated, too, that she didn't want a public memorial service. She requested cremation and asked that her ashes be interned in the family plot beside her two husbands and Lilly and Rosie.

Though Moriah was a remarkably modest, unassuming woman, she knew that she had probably nailed a Nobel Prize. Should she not live to collect it, her will left the money to Rachel. Accompanying the will was a hand written note from Moriah to her friend: "That much money won't fit into your kettle, dear. But I trust that you'll see to its distribution to those most in need."

Charles Newton and the *New York Times* hit the ground running. I thought that another Pulitzer in his pocket was probably a slam dunk. I would be happy for him. My own book, *You May or May Not be Crazy,* was going through the roof again, headed for the stratosphere this time, in sales.

Rachel and I had a lover's *moment,* and we decided that we had fallen in love. Good thing, I thought, for she told me that she was pregnant.

Shortly after Christmas, we contacted authorities and told them that we had Morgan and that he was safe. Rachel bypassed foster home notions and adopted the boy outright with no difficulty whatsoever. We called a Justice of the Peace to the inn and married on New Year's Day.

I sold my cabin on Roubidoux Creek. My new bride and I thought that, when dogwood began to bloom in the spring, we would arrange to get the inn's exterior a badly needed facelift, though she had no intention of reopening it for business. We thought, too, that the lane to the inn should be cleared once more, granting us a more traversable entrance as well as for an occasional visitor.

The city of Hawkins Mill, having been willed Moriah's home, decided to maintain her property for tourists. The house and her belongings would remain undisturbed. Rachel said that her bell ringing days were over. She donated the iconic kettle and bell. They were placed in the small foyer of Moriah's home—*bolted* to a table, actually, lest they become too tempting as souvenirs—where visitors could give whatever they wished. The proceeds would be used to keep the property up.

Dr. von Kepler returned to Heidelberg, Germany. He would meet up with us in Stockholm at Nobel time.

When the concert had ended and choir vanished, Hannah along with them, we wondered if and when we would see her again. She appeared beside me and Rachel on New Year's Day when we took our vows, albeit unseen by the Justice of the Peace. Morgan was permitted to see her, of course, she being his sister, a revelation that we had disclosed to the boy shortly after the concert. "Awesome!" he had said.

Hannah showed up at the inn rather regularly. Rachel sewed Morgan a monk's robe identical to Hannah's. She and her brother enjoyed each other's company very much and explored the forest together. They watched the Chiefs on T.V. Morgan had his pizza and pop. Hannah, being nuclear powered, needing nothing to eat or drink, of course. Rachel asked the girl why she had hit the high C that blew out the street light during the concert. Hannah said she just couldn't help herself.

As the Ozarks began to slowly emerge from winter and reach for spring and summer, the finest news of all was data coming from those whose job it is to keep track of such things: reports of child abuse were down significantly and falling steadily. We thought that this would very much please Moriah and Missymammy. Rachel and I wondered, though, with tongue in cheek, how much of the decline was due to remorse—or, fear that Missymammy might show up at the abuser's door.

Rachel gave birth to a healthy baby girl in July. We named her Rosilee; Rosie for short. She favors her mother, promising another beauty for the Ozark Mountains. As for me, I'm still Evan Van Clevin anyway you cut it. And I owe Cupid an apology.

CPSIA information can be obtained
at www.ICGtesting.com
Printed in the USA
LVOW12s1206060717

540419LV00001BA/27/P